BURYING BETTY

LEE BURTO

BURYING BETTY LEE BERTO

Stories

Wendy Madar

LYCHGATE

BURYING BETTY LEE BERTO

Lychgate Press
First U. S. edition

Distributed by Partners West
Bellingham, Washington

ISBN 13: 978-0-9882887-5-1
ISBN 10: 0-9882887-5-3

Library of Congress Control Number: 2014922011

Corvallis, Oregon
editor@lychgatepress. com
www. lychgatepress. com
Cover design by W. L. Gilroy

For Virginia McCarl Gilroy
Who would have understood these stories all too well

with grateful acknowledgment of my trusted readers
Duncan Thomas, Scott Gilroy, and Jane McCauley Thomas

and also with enduring appreciation for the
Center for the Humanities
Oregon State University

CONTENTS

Burying Betty Lee Berto

In life, Betty Lee Berto was not the sort of person I generally know or want to know, although during the few months of our acquaintance before she died we shared some good laughs. As Betty would have said, she could make the dead guy laugh at a funeral. No one laughed at Betty's funeral. We were all working too hard, the men sweating even though they started digging early to beat the heat.

Because of what happened after Betty died and the unlikely part I ended up playing, I want to make clear that I am no sort of do-gooder, at least not in the usual sense of reading to the blind, visiting old folks I don't know, or volunteering in a soup kitchen. It would be dishonest for me to read to shut-ins because I would have to pretend to like them when, in fact, I care for hardly anyone other than my children, my husband, and a few friends who hang in there despite neglect—I don't have time, with my family, gardening, and reading. I'm not opposed to good works, I'm opposed to lying. Much better to write a check to Community Outreach and leave the hand-holding to those who feel real sympathy and even love for their own kind, no matter how sickly and damaged.

Betty Lee Berto would have laughed if I tried to hold her blue-veined hand, which I saw for the first time lying on top of her thin hospital bedcover. The other hand, I learned soon enough, was under the blanket hiding a pack of Camels. "I love camels, that nice crisp cough you get," were her first words to me as I looked at her from a groggy distance.

There were only two of us in the room. I had just had a routine surgery that's not important to this story. Betty was recovering from a mild stroke that had left no damage that I could see. Her small, blue, heavy-lidded eyes under thin eyebrows drawn on with a pencil counted up my parts from top to toe as the nurses settled me in bed, and as soon as they had gone, she leaned to offer me a smoke, heedless of how this exposed the hanging flesh of her arms, the deflated breasts, the black armpit hairs that I didn't really need to see to disbelieve her yellow head.

"Don't tell me you're a health nut," she said, the cigarette bouncing on her lip as she struck a match with no attempt to hide the sound or the flame. "Camels are the only thing keeping me alive, if they only knew it. And bourbon. You didn't bring a bottle? Well, there's no harm asking. My daddy always said, 'Ask and you won't get it. ' And we didn't, not from him anyway. But the world isn't my daddy, thank Christ for small favors. What did they do, take out your baby plumbing? If I'd had mine out fifty years ago, things would've been different, but I never ask for thanks and damn lucky, too. You don't see me crying."

She laughed, smoke shot out of her mouth and nostrils, she bent double coughing, and two aides rushed in.

By the time we were sent home two days later, I knew Betty's life from her tough roots on a Georgia farm to the defections of all but one of her four children. Or so I was led to believe, and would have continued to believe to this day, except that my little stack of *Fine Gardening* and *New Yorker* magazines ended up going home in Betty's pink overnight bag—I now think she put them there on purpose to give herself an excuse to call—and within a week we met again at her urging. I didn't care about the magazines but I was entertained by her stories and for several months we met irregularly for coffee and further installments on her harrowing history, most often stories about her service in "the second big one " as a WAC. *Take it from me, darlin', if you want a good time, there's nothing like being a soldier.*

2

Except that, when the crisis came, there was no Veteran's burial allowance because there was no record that Betty Lee Berto had ever spent a day in the U. S. military. The only thing that turned out to be true in all her tales was that her favorite daughter, Marie, had not only stayed in touch—unlike the other *ungrateful little bastards*—but made good by succeeding at her own catering business.

So much for my real knowledge of Betty's life. What I do know about is her death.

It was Roberto who told me she had died. He knocked at my door early on an August morning, but of course I didn't know it was Roberto. Betty had never mentioned Roberto. Or Stretch. Or Shine. She had mentioned her husband, Pops, but never by his proper name of Carl. He was always Pops or the Old Man, these spoken with the only tenderness I ever heard from Betty.

But I need to introduce these strange souls to you just as I met them.

Roberto, as I said, was the first. Slight and serious in thick glasses, he stood on my doorstep trembling. "Betty died last night," he said, the words distorted by emotion. "Betty died last night. Betty Lee Berto. Pops is in bad shape."

I never did discover why Roberto came to me. In the strangeness of the moment and the days to follow, it didn't occur to me to ask. But here he was, so I gave him coffee in the dining room while I finished getting my two youngest off to their sports program and prepared to go with Roberto, for that was clearly what he wanted. To do what, I had no idea, but he was so sure I would hurry away with him that I didn't think of refusing.

As we loaded Roberto's heavy three-speed bike into my van I asked whether Betty's children had been told yet.

"I don't know." With a little sobbing breath.

I knew that Betty lived between the highway and the river but was surprised when Roberto directed me into the public housing project just south of the bridge, and as I parked between a dusty station wagon and a pickup with cardboard taped over the passenger's side window, I went hot all over. This was not my world. I had never set foot in a housing project in my life. On three sides we were corralled by two-story green apartment blocks with dirty windows. Hard-used plastic toys lay scattered across brittle remnants of a lawn. What was I to do here?

"If it wasn't for Betty and Pops, I'd still be under the bridge," Roberto said, his eyes big and wet behind the thick lenses. "Me and Stretch and Shine. We're all the same. If it wasn't for Betty—"

Overcome, he bent his head, but soon straightened to lead the way to a door under the open metal stairs. We stepped into air so dark and thick, I thought for a wild moment that Betty was still in the apartment, dead and already decomposing. In the dim green light, three figures sat as still as furniture and I understood from Roberto's reaction that nothing had changed here since he left. The old man looked very bad, his long hair hanging over his face in yellow and white strings, body hunched forward in the armchair like a dummy propped up, hands limp between scrawny thighs, eyes lodged deep under one line of brow. His nose ran in a shiny streak across his mouth and down his chin.

"Pops," Roberto said and knelt by the old man's feet. "Pops. I brought that lady."

He did not seem to hear, and Roberto, gentle as a kitten, drew a wadded cloth from his pocket and wiped the old nose and chin.

"That's Shine, there," he said to me with a sideways dip of the head. "And Stretch. We're all the same. We didn't have nothing."

Shine was in the other armchair leaning back, eyes closed, hands folded on a metal crutch that lay across the chair arms above his legs. Only one foot rested in front of the chair. Beside it hung an empty pant leg.

Stretch lay on the love seat, his long legs pulled up so that his body was jammed between the padded ends like a huge baby in a box. His eyes were open wide and looking at me.

"They took her away," he said, and struggled to sit up, his big head

4

heavy on a neck and torso that looked thin and stretched, worthy of his name. "Pops fought them but they took her."

"They got to take them," Roberto said. "I told you that. That's their job."

"Where did they take her?" I hardly knew what I was saying. What was I supposed to do with this trio of freaks sitting in the smelly half-light, surrounded by beer cans and spilling ash trays? I should be in the garden now doing my daily rounds before the heat settled in. I always take my second cup of coffee in the garden unless it's raining hard.

"Funeral home. I guess." Stretch let his head sag sideways and rested a tear-streaked cheek on his hand.

"Which funeral home?"

"There's more than one?"

"Two. I think." I'd never had anything to do with a funeral home but I'd seen at least two in town. "Does Carl know?"

Carl turned his head, slowly as though it hurt, and looked at me for the first time.

"It was a ambulance," Roberto said. "They took her in a ambulance. There was a fire engine too. And a cop car."

"You're sure she was dead?"

"Carl found her in there." Roberto nodded toward the dark hall and then, his mouth twitching, looked at the thin green drapes that covered the only window in the room, a sliding glass door. "I could open up them curtains."

Briefly stalled like the rest of them, I said nothing and he didn't move. Was there something I was supposed to do? On the drive over, Roberto had tried to tell me something about a funeral but I had not got it and assumed that Carl or one of the children would clue me in. No one close to me had died and I knew nothing of funerals, not even how many days generally pass between death and burial. My parents joked about being tossed onto the compost pile when the time came, but I knew their wills said cremation.

"I could make some coffee," I said.

Roberto nodded with grave agreement as though we had solved a difficult question, and led the way to the little kitchen on the other side of the counter. Working together in the half-light, we assembled coffee powder, creamer, sugar, a kettle. The refrigerator was empty except for a bottle of mineral water, mustard, and dry cat food in a plain plastic bag. A cozy homemaker Betty was not, but someone had kept the place running. A clean dish towel hung on the inside of the cupboard below the sink although I found no dish detergent for the dirty coffee cups.

"She used that powdered kind," Roberto said and waved at the front door, by which I gathered that he meant laundry soap, and the laundry was out there somewhere.

I set coffee on the chair arm next to Carl but he didn't appear to notice. Stretch took his cup in two hands and hung his face in the steam. Shine sipped, sighed, closed his eyes and set the cup on the lamp table without looking so that it knocked beer cans over, which made Carl mutter.

"You drink it," Roberto said and urged his coffee on me, but I could not have put anything in my mouth. It was difficult enough to breathe. Surely the old man wasn't that old, to have wet his pants.

"What about his kids, Roberto? They have to be told. Has someone told them?"

Just Marie, he said. The woman next door had called her but she had to drive from someplace pretty far and would be a while.

The reliable daughter Marie would be here soon. Thank god. My role was now clear. All I had to do was locate Betty's body and get a message to Marie after she arrived so that she could proceed with funeral arrangements. Even Carl nodded as I said I was going back to my house to call the funeral homes in order to find Betty, and Stretch gave a forlorn little smile. I fled into fresh air.

My first call was to the county emergency services but the ambulance run had been too recent for it to have been entered on the log book and

6

no one was able to recall picking up a dead old woman.

"It's been a busy morning," the dispatcher said, brisk and happy.

Next I tried St. Mary's hospital as I had a vague memory that even dead people are taken first to an emergency room, just to be sure. Sorry, said the desk. We're not allowed to give out patient information except to relatives.

"She's not a patient. She's dead."

That Betty was dead made no difference. The woman would tell me nothing even when I explained the situation right down to Shine's missing leg. Such mindless failure to help was puzzling and disappointing. I assumed that, once told the particulars, anyone would understand and would do the reasonable thing, and I continued to believe this for a surprisingly long time. The Bertos needed help. It was so obvious.

The call to St. Mary's did help in one regard—it made me cagey. Next calling the police, I claimed to be a niece and was told that Betty had been taken by ambulance to Niels Johnson Funeral Home. Triumphant, I called the funeral home instead of simply passing the information along to Marie, but when Niels Johnson came on the line I found myself at a loss. What is the proper way to refer to a corpse? Should I ask whether Betty Lee Berto was at the funeral home or Betty Lee Berto's body? I needn't have worried. As soon as I mentioned Berto, Johnson took over.

"I'm so glad you called. Mrs. Berto is here with us. I was just trying to find a number for Mr. Berto. There is a Mr. Berto?" These things need to be taken care of quickly, he said, difficult as they are for everyone. He realized that Mr. Berto would be grieving, and this is always particularly hard on the elderly, but then so many of them are elderly, but he understood there were several children and sometimes it helps the family to be involved because it gives them one last loving thing to do for their loved ones. And could I please give him the names and numbers of the other surviving kin?

He didn't believe me at first when I said I had no idea who or where any of the children were except that a daughter named Marie was on her way to town. When he asked for my address and telephone number, I said I would not be involved after today except to attend the funeral. Well, he said, you're obviously an important friend to be trusted with helping at such a time and I'd like to be sure you receive an announcement.

"Announcement?"

Yes, he said, most people like to send announcements to close friends and relatives. Like weddings.

"I have a feeling they won't be doing that," I said, and he made a little humming noise.

After a stout cup of coffee, I returned to the apartment. A thin woman with puffy eyes met me at the door, threw her arms around me, and dragged me inside.

"I'm Marie," she said. "Roberto told me you were helping out. Thank you, thank you so much. I'm Marie Kinney, hardly the oldest but I might as well be. I just finished calling the others but I don't expect it will make any difference. Except for Davie. He'll be here. But I had to call them anyhow, didn't I?"

"The other two can't make it for the funeral?"

"Two? You mean seven. There was nine, counting me and Davie, but I guess they hardly add up to more than about two real ones. They're mostly Carl's." Fresh tears gushed as she whispered, "I want the best for mother."

The apartment had changed during my brief absence. Not only were the drapes open wide but the cans, bottles, and ashtrays were gone and so were Carl, Shine, Stretch, and Roberto, along with their shoes and other leavings. I could hear the shower and guessed that Marie had moved Carl in there. I didn't ask about Roberto and the others. This was clearly Marie's show now and the sight of everything tidied and brightened up, and the realization that I was off the hook and could go home, made me feel warm toward this sharp-chinned young woman. Betty had talked about her with pride.

"Her own business. She's the boss. But that's no surprise. She used to boss me and Carl around!"

Taking Marie's hand, feeling almost tearful myself suddenly, I said I was so sorry about Betty. "I didn't know your mother well but she talked about you with great fondness. Please let me know about the funeral."

Marie's hand went tight as a clamp and her eyes opened wide. "But you're going with us. I never did this before and I want to do it right. Carl said he wouldn't go and I said he had to. Roberto said you would."

Niels Johnson shook my hand and held Marie's as he nodded at Carl. "Mr. Berto. I'm so sorry about your wife."

Carl wore a white shirt that Marie had ironed on the table but there had been no clean pants to be found, so he wore the old ones, sponged clean and belted up tight. Marie had helped him shave and combed his hair back with water. He didn't say anything to Niels Johnson. He sat back in the wooden armchair and looked at the ceiling with his eyes in slits.

Marie and I sat on one side of the shiny table and Niels Johnson sat on the other, hands folded on some papers. Worn from the strain of the odd day and not feeling connected with the proceedings, I looked at the wall and wondered how far away Betty lay, whether she was already in a coffin or had been tucked up in a drawer, and what it would do to a person to work in such a gilt and brocade palace of the dead year after year. A shriek snapped me back to attention.

Carl was on his feet, his hawk eyes fixed on Johnson, two bony fists shaking in rage. "You can just forget cremation!"

"Mr. Berto. Please. I understand your feelings. This is a very difficult time for everyone concerned and we all want to do what's right. But you have to understand that funerals cost money. They are not a public service. Your daughter tells me there isn't a lot of money and I'm trying to give her cheaper options. Cremation is the cheapest way—stop, please—it's cheap but perfectly respectable. You'd be surprised at the people who choose cremation. People who could afford the best of everything."

"Carl," said Marie. "Carl, you can sit down. We won't let them cremate Mother no matter what. We'd like to see the caskets now."

Soft music played in the room where a dozen huge jewel boxes waited with open lids that showed linings in baby blue and rose satin. Embarrassed as though we were shopping for sex props, I stepped away from the others. A casket with a forest scene painted on the underside of the lid stopped me, and I might have laughed except that Marie had followed and now touched a tender hand to the gold satin rim.

"Mother loved trees. Didn't mother love trees, Carl?"

Carl said nothing. He had remained by the door where he stood looking at his shoes.

"How much is this one?"

Niels Johnson's voice was hushed as he praised her choice, but rather than saying the price, he lifted a tag for her to see. Twenty-two hundred. Marie flinched and blinked, and we moved away from the casket with the forest scene.

"Perhaps there is something. If you'd come this way please?" Johnson led us out of the casket room, down the mauve-carpeted hallway, through a heavy door, down plain wooden stairs to a basement, through a room where lumber was stacked, and into a small, cold room with shelves to the ceiling. On the shelves were long coffins of plain pressboard, the edges sharp and the hinges showing.

"These are only a hundred and fifty," he said. "But we can't allow viewing in them."

"I'm not having my mama put under the ground without seeing her one last time!"

Johnson looked at his watch.

"You don't have anything else? I have to see my mama. I didn't get to say goodbye and I have to say goodbye. I don't care what else. What about that one?" Marie pointed to a lone box in the corner. It was as plain and square as the pressboard caskets but was covered in thin gray cloth.

"That's the last one. We stopped stocking those. It's three hundred. You can view in that but that's the limit."

"I'll take it then." Marie turned without looking at him and strode upstairs. She headed for the double front doors but Johnson called her back. A great deal remained to be done, he said, many decisions to be made. We filed again into the meeting room. Grim and determined, Marie gripped my forearm with one hand under the table as she bartered with Johnson over the laying out, viewing, flowers, announcements. . . . Again my thoughts wandered. This time I was jerked back to the present by Marie, who leaped to her feet so violently she knocked her chair over. "You're just going to leave my mama laying there?" she shouted.

"That's not what I said." Niels Johnson also stood up, his face red. "I said you have to give me half the money before the funeral. That's nothing out of the ordinary. Don't you have to make a down payment before you buy furniture or a car? Why do people think funerals are any different. You're buying our services. How do I know I'll get paid after it's over? We can't exactly repossess a body."

He had gone too far. With a gasp, Marie recoiled as though from poison and rushed for the door. Johnson circled the table fast to intercept her.

"Let's hold on here a minute, let's just take it easy. I'm not a bad guy, I want to help. I know you're upset about your mother. These are always difficult times for the family. I just can't believe that none of you have money, not with nine kids. Just ask your brothers and sisters. Get each one to put in some. It's only two hundred each, and that will buy your mother a funeral you can feel proud of the rest of your life. You don't want to have regrets."

Marie had kept walking as he talked and went out the door without answering, leaving me to collect Carl and say parting words to Niels Johnson, which I managed well enough—Betty's body, after all, was here and had to be dealt with—but without apologizing for Marie's behavior. We found her standing by the car sobbing and swearing, but she opened the door for Carl and slid into the driver's seat with matter-of-fact movements, as though tears weren't drenching her cheeks.

"I wouldn't say it to that cretin, but I'll tell you. The rest of them just aren't much good, even Davie. If I don't do it, she won't get any kind of funeral at all. I don't know where I'll get the money."

I could have paid for the funeral. I could have put it on Visa and never known the difference. Why didn't I? It didn't feel like the right thing, that's all I can say. We sat in silence, Carl in back as still and distant as a carving, his hair once again hanging over his face in an inverted V like a tepee.

"And what am I going to do with him?" Marie said, more to herself than to me. "I guess the only thing is to get him some whiskey and get it over with. Damn, damn, damn it to hell. My mama had a hard life, but she wasn't bad. She deserves a decent finish, and I'm not going to put up with any more shit from anybody."

I had to go back to my own life to make dinner but I returned to the apartment in the late evening, by which time Marie had made her plans. She was sitting on a straight chair in front of the sliding glass door while the others were settled in a circle in front of her, Shine, Stretch, Roberto, and Davie, the brother. Everything in Davie's narrow face was wrong— messy teeth, crooked nose, scarred cheek, limp hair—except for his eyes, which were as fresh and blue as any I'd ever seen. Carl, in his chair, no longer stared without seeing but looked around the room at one person after another with a quizzical frown, as though he wanted someone to tell him what was happening but he didn't know how to ask.

"We're putting a collection box at Mike's Tavern," said Marie. "Mother used to go there. She was known there."

"And Pops, too," said Roberto. "They all like Pops."

"I called Reverend Ballard. He promised the church will print the programs. For free. That's not a lot but it will help. Every little bit helps."

To hear that Betty had been a churchgoer was yet another surprise, but I learned later that this had been Marie's church when she was in high school, after she went to live with her girlfriend's family when Carl was locked up for drunk driving. Marie's eyes were red but she talked as though she were planning a trip somewhere, first we do this and then we do that, a little excited and eager. She knew a woman with a flower store who would let her have the flowers for half price if she arranged them herself. The neighbor upstairs had said there was some kind of burial allowance that came with Social Security and she was going to call somebody about that tomorrow. Stretch and Shine and even Davie just watched her, but Roberto kept chiming in with suggestions that she ignored until he said, "Where's she going to be buried at?"

"The cemetery, of course."

"Don't that cost money?"

Marie opened her mouth, stopped, closed her eyes, and shuddered. She looked at Pops and then at me.

"I believe they do charge for burial plots," I said. "Didn't Niels Johnson talk about that?"

"I don't know. I can't remember. He must've said something."

"Why don't I find out for you in the morning?" I said, relieved to have found something simple I could do for her.

Two cemeteries were listed in the phone book. At Grove Lawn, the call was answered by a man who said he couldn't help me because he was the groundskeeper. "I just mow 'em, I don't bury 'em," he said, perfectly serious. A man at Perpetual Harmony said that people buy funeral plots at the cemetery before they die, not afterward. After death, he said, they have to go through a funeral home.

"I told Miss Berto all that." Niels Johnson was impatient, almost irritated. "Why don't you ask her? No, never mind. There's no point if they can't afford a funeral." His voice dropped and his tone turned cautious as he continued, "In this kind of case, they don't always go to a regular cemetery."

I had lived in this community for eighteen years but I had never heard of Hull's Field. I could not believe what Johnson was saying. Hull's Field was a county graveyard—a dumping ground for the dead poor. It was like the movie, *Amadeus*, when they heave Mozart's body from the cart into a communal pit grave and throw lime over him. But this is the 21st century, this is a well-to-do town in Oregon. . . Betty Lee Berto, dyed yellow hair, fake diamond rings, old fur coat, all tumbled into a hole and doused with lime?

Well, it wasn't quite like that. Hull's Field, I discovered when I left Johnson and drove out to find it, was a cemetery with separate plots, but not like any cemetery most of us would recognize. The dirt road north of town wound uphill through a Christmas tree farm and ended at the top in a small gravel parking area next to a sloping field dotted with oaks. There was no sign to mark its purpose. Uncertain, I walked over dry grass that broke like twigs underfoot. The ground was uneven but had I not been told the dead were buried here, I would never have noticed that the humps were of a certain length and width. I might have wondered about the small weathered pieces of board with traces of writing that lay here and there. It was simple, clean, rich with summer field smells, and it seemed not a bad place to end up.

But I couldn't really like it. Walking over the discarded dead, dead who were discards in life, I couldn't like it.

Marie was sick when I told her. Covering her face with her hands, she slumped on the couch and cried yet more tears, but after a bit she lifted her head. "God's outdoors is all the same, I guess. Only I wished it didn't have to be with just poor folks."

When her tears were done, Marie appeared more relieved than disturbed about the gravesite and, encouraged, I decided to pursue other possibilities without telling her, in case they came to nothing. The first thing I discovered was that Betty was no vet, which I might have guessed given that neither Carl nor Marie had mentioned a possible military burial allowance. She had lied to me about all kinds of things, I realized, but it didn't matter. It wasn't personal. Life and performance, there's no difference to some people.

I dropped in at the Community Outreach office to see if they knew of any public program that pays for funerals.

"The state used to help out," I was told by Carmen Blodgett, a big woman with friendly eyes. "They said they need the money to help the living, but what they forget is that it's the living that need help when somebody dies. The dead can't be helped. I don't know if it will do any good, but I'll talk to Johnson. Oh, yes, I know Niels Johnson, you bet I do."

Carmen suggested that, just for the record, I should go over to the welfare office and tell them about it. Maybe if they see there's a real need, she said, they'll do something someday. I had never been in a welfare office and never expected to be in a welfare office. I sat in my car across the street for ten minutes, then walked briskly in, with purpose.

"The Bertos?" The woman behind the desk laughed. "It's nice of you to help out but you should know they've taken this state for every service we offer and then some. You can't save people from themselves. I'm sorry for Marie. She was always a good kid, the only one that had any sense in the whole lot. She was lucky to get out when she did or she might have ended up like the others. I don't think a single one of them ever held down a job more than a week. People have done more than enough for that crew. Anyway, there's no program support for that kind of thing, for funerals and what have you."

Marie managed to collect $735, less than half what was needed. Davie came up with fifty somewhere, which she could hardly believe, and kept asking him, Are you sure this is your money? None of the other kids showed up or communicated with Marie.

"What am I going to do—my mama's laying there waiting!" She demanded with fierce despair. "I'm going to see Johnson, to see what we can do. No, you don't have to come. I'm mad enough now to do it on my own."

"I'll go, "I said again. "It's better to have two."

I don't know whether it was because of Carmen Blodgett's call, or a particularly good lunch, or he simply saw that there was no more to be got out of this family and he had a corpse on his hands, but Niels Johnson said he would do the funeral for $735. I thought for a moment that Marie might rush around the table and embrace him, but then he dropped the bomb.

"You'll never get a grave digger to work half price. You'll have to dig it yourself."

Marie went rigid. I grabbed her arm because I saw it jerk as though she might punch him, but she didn't move and remained silent for so long that Johnson shifted in his chair and thumbed his papers uneasily.

"I'm not ashamed to dig my own mama's grave," she said at last, and marched out like a regiment.

On Saturday morning I drove the men out to Hull's Field in my van. Marie said she couldn't stand to see the grave being dug after all and would do the flowers. I decided to help her rather than stay with Roberto and the others, so I didn't see the grave until the service was over and they took Betty out there, the hearse sliding in under the oaks like a great black beetle.

We walked down the dry, grassy slope, Roberto, Stretch, Davie, Carl, and an old fellow Betty knew at Mike's Tavern carrying the coffin. Shine hobbled along with just one crutch so he could at least keep a hand on the box. And a box was just what it looked like, a big gray shoebox with a bunch of white flowers on top. The grave was surrounded by heaped yellow clay that appeared to have exploded out of the hole. Balancing on the clods, the men lowered Betty into the hole with two short lengths of rope.

Nothing remained to be done except to cover her up.

"Goodbye, Mama," Marie whispered, and then fell to the ground in a faint when Davie threw in a clump of clay that boomed hollow on the coffin. She soon came around and I led her back to the car while the men filled in the grave. When they all trooped back up, sweating and silent, Marie said she wanted to go back down to say a last goodbye. I went with her, holding her arm, and we stood there in the sun and looked at the white dahlias that sagged against the plastic cross. I cried then, too. I remembered Betty's mocking wit and her ridiculous painted eyebrows.

"She wasn't what you call a real good person," said Marie. "But she wasn't bad. She was my own mama."

Marie went home to her business in Washington. Carl stayed in his apartment at the project. Now that I know them, I see Shine and Stretch around town now and then, Shine swinging along on his crutches with the loose pant leg that won't stay pinned flopping under him, while Stretch shuffles alongside, taking baby steps with his giraffe legs to keep pace with Shine. As for Roberto, he turned up at my house one more time, with a letter for me to read. It was addressed to state Senator Linda Mackey.

"I got her name from this guy down at Mike's. He said you got to start off 'Dear Senator Mackey' and then tell what you want. So that's how I done it."

The letter was a mess of misspellings and mistakes, but it told Betty's story right through to the digging of the grave, and ended by saying that something should be done to help "poor people get buried right and not just treated like garbage. Betty Lee Berto wasn't perfect but I would still be under the bridge doing nothing if it wasn't for her, instead of working a job and paying taxes too. She was real people."

This, I should say, was how it read after I retyped it. I didn't ask about the job. Roberto pulled out a wallet and extrcted a single stamp.

"I got this special," he said. He folded the letter and put it in the envelope and was about to lick the flap.

"Did you sign it?"

"Oh, right. I forgot." He picked up a pencil from the table but I suggested a pen. He held the pen tight and sat for a while before writing with slow care, and then sat back with a smile that made his gold tooth flash.

Roberto Juan Camacho Muñoz.

I said he could put the letter in my mailbox and it would be picked up today but he said no, he thought he'd ride on down to the post office and give it to somebody there.

"Just to be sure," he said. "Nothing against you."

He pedaled away on his white bike with the fat tires, and that was the last I saw of him. But he stayed around town like the others. I know this because yesterday he was found dead of heart failure in Mary's River Park. A small story in today's paper said no one knows where he lived but several downtown merchants praised him. He was always polite, they said, and he collected bottles to get money to feed cats under the bridge. Only the clerk at the Food-Mart was unsympathetic.

"He had a wife and four kids down at Salinas. He told me he did. He never even wrote."

The story said nothing about a funeral service.

Finished with the newspaper and coffee, I rolled the trash cart down the driveway to the curb for pick up. It wouldn't be April for a few days yet, but the indigo salvia in the flowerbed that bordered the drive was pushing new leaves into the light and so were half a dozen other perennials that needed dividing or trimming. Usually I do this in fall as part of the general garden cleanup, but I'd read a letter in a gardening magazine that said the writer had had better luck with survival not pruning her perennials until early spring.

Kneeling at the edge of the flowerbed with my gloves and clippers, I counted eighteen tulips about to open. I hadn't gone back to Hull's Field since Betty was buried, but now I knew what to do. When the tulips bloomed, I would cut them all and put them on Betty's grave. She wouldn't mind that they were meant for Roberto.

Breaking the Window

The night Mac didn't come home from work and didn't call to say why, Denise remained calm almost through dinner, which she prepared and served late after she realized that something out of the ordinary, and most likely nasty, had penetrated the family battlements. Awkward in the kitchen that had become Mac's territory since she went back to teaching, she boiled noodles and made three salad plates of lettuce, green pepper cut in rings, and canned pineapple.

Where was Mac? The drive home from work was just fifteen miles, he had a spare tire, and she would have heard by now had anything serious happened. It wasn't his staff meeting day. He had said nothing about a parent conference, and he never stayed after school for his own purposes. He fled at the precise minute allowed by contract, half an hour after the bell rang. Even though her school was closer, he was always home by the time she arrived, always in his chair in a sacred circle of newspapers, ashtray, sherry, and library books that would carry him through the evening while she graded papers and steered the boys through homework and baths.

Dinner, such as it was, was ready but Denise did not call the children. She poured white wine and stood looking out the window at the cows filing along Nordberg's fence in the twilight, going to be milked as they did every day, twice a day, days without end. How exquisite the land was in the evening, purple and green and flat as Holland, with the fields and lowing cows, and an echo of sunset touching with mauve everything from the gray fence posts to the lone cottonwood tree that stood where two fence lines met. How Mac had raved about the view when they found this place, while she had stopped inside the front door, unable to believe that anyone would put red linoleum on a living room floor.

Look at the view, he had urged as he stood by a tall window that showed dairy fields rolling to green horizon. *It could be the prairies.*

It's windy enough, she had said, wishing for beauty indoors as well as out, but taken, even so, with the idea of two school teachers living in an old country schoolhouse with the belfry intact and a big wooden platform out back for the kids to play on when the low fields turned sloppy. Long and narrow, with high ceilings and many close-set windows, the two-room school had been divided into six deep rooms as tall as they were wide and full of blank daylight. In early evening, the rooms on the west side colored briefly with gold and rose, and then Denise would sit in her armchair and let the rich hues of sunset cleanse her of the cumulative insult of the day, the tide of uncaring ignorance that she fought as though to save the lives of these sons and daughters of the soil.

Turning from the window to the sink, Denise held her hands under hot water and shuddered as heat loosened her cold fingers and swept up her arms. She had been right, the wind did blow out here on the valley floor day and night, right through the cracked putty and warped frames of the original sash windows. Her hands were always cold. Cold. Quaint. They had come to mean the same thing over the years of their marriage—quaint, cold, and as poor as the country school teachers they were. They had made their choices and Mac seemed happy enough with the result, although a good deal less dedicated to his students than she was. She couldn't leave the classroom behind her as he did every night, as though it didn't exist. She struggled and planned and searched for lively material. There had to be a way to get through to them about

Faulkner and Welty. Hemingway they could get, at least at some level, but what did Hemingway give them?

"Don't agonize over it," Mac advised, his feet working inside his socks on the hassock as they so often did, flexing like independent live things that seemed disconnected from the calm, instructive voice—the voice of a *reasonable man* as he would have described it. "Something is bound to rub off on them. If you look at it historically, if you consider the centuries of illiteracy stretching back into human history, it's amazing that most students today can actually read. Whether they do much of it is another question."

She was not persuaded that he believed in this minimalist view, but she had given up arguing.

Surely, wherever he was, he should have called by now. It's a simple courtesy to let your family know where you are. He was not a man to hang out with his buddies—he had no buddies. He was a man who came home after work, cooked dinner, and read until he was ready to sleep.

"Joey!" she called, and then, seeing the dining room through the eyes of her children, she was appalled at the ugliness of the hardening cheese and noodle casserole and the three plates of pineapple and soft lettuce under white ceiling light. There was no lamp in the little dining area between the kitchen and living room but there were candles in the utensil drawer. Denise opened the heavy drawer, lifted slotted spoons, a spatula, a can opener, and took out two ends of white candle. She put them on saucers in puddles of wax, turned off the overhead light, and called to the boys.

"This pineapple tastes like tin," Charlie said and spit it onto his plate. "Where's Dad?

The telephone rang. No one moved. It rang again, and then a third time. Charlie and Denise pushed away from the table at the same instant.

"I'll get it," Denise said, but Charlie continued toward the kitchen counter as though he hadn't heard.

"Don't touch that phone."

Charlie reached for the receiver.

"Charles!"

His hand suspended, Charlie turned to his mother as the telephone rang a fourth time. "You never get the phone."

"I'll answer it." Waving her son back to the table, Denise lifted the receiver and heard a man's voice.

"Mrs. Hazel? I have your husband here."

"Who's speaking, please?"

"Don't be coy, Mrs. Hazel. You know me."

"If you wish to speak to me you will say who you are."

A low chuckle came over the line, intimate and wet sounding. "Very well, Mrs. Hazel. I'll play your game. This is Master Tod Jonson, a madman who masquerades as a teacher. I'm calling on behalf of your jovial husband the Right Honorable Maximillian Hazel the Cloven-Hoofed."

"Really."

"I think you should know that Mac is having a lovely time here at Freddie's with his friends."

"Really."

"The thing about friends, Mrs. Hazel, is that they don't act like they own you. They don't demand to know where you are twenty-four hours a day. Mrs. Hazel? You aren't very talkative. Shall I tell your husband you don't care for his friends?"

"Go to hell."

Wine splashed onto the counter as Denise poured, wondering that she felt no urge to cry, just a deep cold anger. Or was it disgust? Or maybe it was plain disappointment that made her insides squeeze and her hand shake. She should have guessed—of course it was Tod Jonson's doing. *He's a rough cob but funny as hell*, Mac had said when Jonson joined the teaching staff in the fall. *He tells me he likes to break up marriages. Not your usual hobby!*

"Was that Dad? Did you say go to hell?"

24

"It was just a crank call, Joey. Nothing to worry about."

"Mom, are you drunk?"

"Drunk? Do you think I'm drunk? I am not drunk," she said, amazed. "I am never drunk. Your father is drunk."

"I thought so!" Joey almost sang the words. "That's what Darin's dad does. He gets smashed and they save his dinner and he eats it for breakfast."

The boys laughed, wild and shrill.

"It's too dark in here." Charlie hopped to his feet and turned on the overhead light.

Joey cleared the table without being asked.

After dinner, Charlie disappeared into his room but Joey settled in the living room, lying on his stomach on the couch writing out algebra equations while Denise drank wine and smoked. A silent hour passed before she said, deliberate and almost savoring, "If your father isn't home in half an hour I'm going to throw this bottle through that window."

"What?" Joey twisted to look at his mother in the green armchair where she sat every night grading papers or reading. She was not grading or reading now.

"If your father isn't home in half an hour, I'm going to throw this bottle through that window."

"Where is Dad?"

"Playing the fool, to use one of his favorite expressions. But I am not a fool's wife." Denise drank from the glass in her right hand and Joey saw then that her other hand rested on a slim green bottle that sat on the chair beside her.

"Don't throw it with your left hand," he said. Shocked by his own words, he searched his mother's face for disapproval.

She laughed, short and sharp. "I won't. Thank you for the advice, sweetie pie."

"Is he alone?"

"What do you think?"

25

"He's with somebody because he'd get bored drinking by himself. Maybe that teacher with the funny accent."

"How right you are." Denise regarded her eldest son with uneasy pride in his powers of perception. How had he guessed? How much did he know? Of course, the boys had heard Mac talk about Jonson, about his bachelor habits, his scorn for just about everyone, and certainly that terrible story about the mentally handicapped boy who had crawled into his classroom, apparently lost and looking for his own class. Jonson had said, *Somebody throw it a biscuit.*

Throw it a biscuit!

Mac had been outraged. But amused, too, at least a little. *There isn't a truly funny line that isn't cruel to somebody*, he had said. *The best wit is the cruelest. Nobody expects comedians to be saints or saints to be funny.*

What were they doing at Freddie's for all these hours? Mac was not a bar person, never had been a bar person. She could not imagine him in a bar surrounded by noise and bluster and boozy stupidity.

I don't seem to be a proper man at all, he had said more than once, wondering and maybe a little sad. *I have no ambition. Why should I struggle to rise above others? I can't seem to feel proper love—isn't fatherly love supposed to be instinctual? Every year there are kids in my class I like as well as my own. They're just damn good kids and it makes no difference whose seed produced them. Face it, Denise, either I'm a truly rational man or I'm a mistake of nature.*

Denise didn't believe him when he talked like this. It's true that he often failed to show the expected sentiments and yet he had cried on the way to the hospital after Charlie cut his head severely on the playground. Is that what it took to awaken his real emotions? Disaster. Violence. A bottle through the window.

Emotion is primitive, he said. *If reason triumphed over emotion more often we'd live in a better world. I hardly know what people mean when they talk about love and hate. No one is truly lovable. I am not lovable.*

I'm with Groucho on that—I wouldn't want to be in a club with anyone who could love me.

"Well," she had said, "isn't it lucky we're married and not in the Kiwanis."

Looking up at Tod Jonson through the open car window, Mac Hazel took a slow, steadying breath and declaimed from deep in his chest. "'I've left rings of beer on every alehouse table from the Salt Sea coast across half a dozen counties, and every time I thought I was on the way to a faintly festive hiccough, the sight of the damned world sobered me up again!'"

"Sounds like a waste of good drink to me," Jonson said, and called back as he walked away into the night. "Give my love to dear Denise and tell her I enjoyed our little talk."

Mac turned the key hard, stomped the accelerator so that the old Chevy roared like a lion on the kill, shoved the gear stick into drive, and whooped when the car leaped away from the curb and sped up the dark street. What a miracle cars are, so efficient, so powerful, so symbolic of man's incredible dominion over nature. Could an ape design a car? Hell no. It's all very well to teach chimps sign language and marvel that they can ask for an orange, but there's nothing on earth or elsewhere in the universe like the human brain. Cars, plastics, electric light, space shuttle, designer microbes. Human footprints on the goddamned moon—what a privilege it is to be human. Damn these pessimists and their whining about population and pollution and all the other everlasting crises in the world. Damn these doomsayers. He couldn't agree with Tod there, there he went overboard with his contempt, and Mac had let him know it in fine style.

"Think of something original, man!" he'd insisted. "The damn doomsayers were predicting the end of the earth when they still thought it was flat. Man is a problem-solving animal. He fouls his nest and then cleans it out. Man always lands on his feet like a cat. Think of it, the pure, incredible, unheard of ingenuity of the species."

Consider modern roads, he continued in silent argument as he leaned into the curves. What marvelous engineering goes into roads, into bridges and overpasses, tunnels through mountain ranges, intricate networks of freeway junctions, those curved and curlicued arabesques of concrete. How could anyone believe that god invented man—hell, man invents himself!

Chuckling, proud of his kind, Mac cranked the window down, twisted his head to look up at a crowded sky, and then faced straight into the night wind. What a fine thing a deserted highway is. He wished he had more than fifteen miles to go to get home where Denise would be—how had Bobby Burns put it?—*nursin' her wrath to keep it warm*. That was it. But he wouldn't think of that, not now, not yet. Approaching the little store and gas pump at Fernbridge where he would turn off to cross the river he was surprised not to see a single light. The bridge was empty and a smell of water and willows filled the car. It was late, very late, and there was no point hurrying now. Why not walk a little? Why not park at the fishing pullout and walk up the river path under the stars?

Mac was pulling off into the gravel at the end of the bridge when he thought of his shoes, his low-top, polished black teaching shoes. Not a man's shoes. Men wear boots and stride over the earth. Low-top shoes are for women. Thin socks are for women. Bows and ties are for women. Speeding up again, driving one-handed, Mac worked his tie loose, pulled it over his head, and stuffed it in his coat pocket. Jonson refused to wear a tie. Jonson was never late for dinner because dinner was whenever he chose to eat. What did he eat? Mac could not recall having seen Tod eat anything except chocolate bars and peanuts, but of course Tod never ate lunch at school, never went into the coffee room where the shrill babble of women's chatter was enough to give a man a headache. What a relief it had been when Tod was hired, with his rumpled shirt and his habitual scowl. Melva Bowen in the office told everyone Tod slept in his clothes.

28

I can smell him, she sniffed.

When Mac told Tod about it he'd laughed and snorted, *She doesn't know what a real man smells like.*

Mac laughed again, thinking of it. What a great line. Even Denise would see the humor in it.

Denise. Denise.

Mac slowed the car a little, wound up the window, cleared his throat. Surely, Denise would be in bed by now. She would have taken care of dinner and gone to bed, all three of them, the house would be black and silent and he could slip in, have a little snack and then sleep. He was very tired suddenly, his eyes blurring as he watched the white line. She would be in bed but there would be a letter. That was her style, to deal with problems on paper. If only it stopped there it wouldn't be bad, it was civilized to write things down, but she never could leave it at that and would nag at him, not at breakfast because the kids would hear but tomorrow, in the evening, there would be no escaping her. She would want an explanation. But what to explain? Men have always gone out drinking with men. Maybe Tod was right that he she had him by the nose.

Maybe he would bring Tod home with him from work and the two of them could jaw at each other while Mac read. Tod was a match for her, although it's possible that he had overdone it on the phone.

I'll call your wife, he had said suddenly, banging his glass down on the table. He never drank anything but gin. He said beer tastes like convent piss and wine is for invalids.

No need to call, Mac had told him, but Tod was already digging for change in the pocket of his floppy trousers.

Don't want to upset the little woman, he said, showing yellow teeth. *Have to tell mommy where we are.*

The telephone was on the wall far enough from their table so that Mac had to listen hard to make out words. The few he'd heard made him wince and nod at the same time. The man had a wit, a terrible wit, but a wit nonetheless. Nothing thin-blooded about Jonson. That would teach Denise a thing or two. . . it wouldn't hurt at any rate. Surely she knew what to expect, he had told her all about Jonson, she couldn't possibly take a character like that seriously,

Mac turned into the curving gravel drive that, designed for school buses, circled past the house and always gave him just the slightest sense of embarrassed elegance as he pulled in, as though it were lined with stately elms rather than weeds. But what a joke life is! He never had liked school and here he was at forty-two teaching all day and then going home to a schoolhouse, a school teacher wife, and two sons who had spent all day in school. So it went, life just happening to him. Like a rock in a field he endured while rain fell, wind blew, snow piled up, and he didn't know why, didn't know how he ended up here, didn't seem to have made any particular decisions along the way. A career? Ambition? Goals? They were words from a foreign land, a land where men take themselves and life seriously, where they stir around with self-important faces and serve on committees and chase promotions and write outraged letters to the editor.

All he wanted was to be let alone, little enough to ask.

The porch light was on but the rest of the house was dark, the windows black, the treeless yard silent and other-worldly. He didn't know what time it was. He couldn't remember just when the clock in the car had quit, and he would not wear a watch.

"What's time to a hog anyhow?" he said to the silent house, and thought of the alarm set to go off in the gray morning, the stomach and head that would afflict him, the silence of his wife. Hushed, moving like a thief, he eased open the door.

Standing in the living room in his socks, he wondered at the coolness of the house. It was almost breezy. He listened and heard nothing. They slept, all three, and thinking of them lying passive, unconscious, his two boys and his wife, Mac nodded in the dark. Yes. He liked them this way quite well. They were a solid fact, two children and a wife, they were

30

evidence of something, proof of something.

But where was Denise's letter? On his chair? He would have to turn on a light. But maybe he wouldn't. Maybe he would just go to bed without any fuss or searching or reading. Maybe he would just drink some water and then sink into the brief sleep that would be allowed him, and face her fury tomorrow rather than reading about it tonight. He couldn't imagine what she would write, he had never done anything quite like this before, this drinking late in a bar with Jonson.

How had she taken Tod's call? Was she really sleeping now? Sleep was generally the first thing to go when Denise was upset and she might even now be standing in the hall.

Uneasy, Mac snapped on a lamp and saw a living room in perfect order, the little rug straight in front of the couch, the books in two neat stacks by his chair, Denise's ashtray not only emptied but wiped clean. There was no letter—good lord, the window. The center pane of the second window was a jagged black hole that let in a whisper of night air. He nodded at this revelation of the source of the chill in the house even as he crossed to examine the hole. He tried to look through to see if the answer might lie outside but could see nothing. There was no glass on the floor so the window must have been broken from inside. Charlie's basketball. Or the boys wrestling—how many times had he sent them out of the living room for failing to act civilized. Irritated, Mac thought of having to measure, order glass, chip out old glazing, putty the thing in place, clean the new glass so it wouldn't look amateurish.

Well, he'd let the boys do it. They were old enough now for such tasks and they might think twice next time before flinging themselves around the house like untrained puppies. But still there was no letter. There was no letter, the house was silent as death, and the impossibility had to be faced: the broken window was the letter. The broken window, as unheard of in their married world as staying out at a bar with an oaf like Jonson, was Denise's statement of protest.

Mac shook his head. No. Denise was not the window breaking type, and most certainly not with the children at home. He hadn't considered what she might say to the boys when he didn't come home, didn't show up to cook dinner, didn't call to let them know he had not driven over a cliff. Denise must have cooked and they all sat down together and talked about. . . what?

What if Tod's call had come as they all sat there, the phone sitting on the counter and any conversation being audible from the table.

Tired, cold, disturbed by thoughts of what the boys might have heard, Mac felt an unaccustomed discomfort in his stomach and thought suddenly that he had not eaten dinner, had eaten nothing but peanuts since lunch. He went to the refrigerator to look for the remains of the meal that had left a lingering smell in the cold house, something cheesy he guessed. The bowl on the top shelf was covered with a plate. Setting the bowl on the counter, he extracted a fork from the dish rack without making a sound, removed the plate, and found a folded piece of paper.

The letter was in the bowl.

As relieved as though a loose snake had been located in the dark, he unfolded the unlined sheet. It was blank. He turned it over. Blank again.

"Hell!" What was wrong with the woman?

Crumpling the paper, Mac pushed it into his trouser pocket and went wearily down the hall. Tod Jonson would be sleeping by now, lying in his shirt and shorts on the bed that was just as he had left it that morning, no blank note in his pocket, no broken window, no woman's fury to be faced in the morning.

Women have no sense of humor.

That was it, that was exactly it! Surprised by insight, Mac stopped outside the bedroom door and considered what life would be like if women—wives—had a sense of humor, if Denise had simply joked with Tod when he called, had left a funny note on the counter along with a bit of dinner, had realized, in short, that this little side trip meant nothing at all, was only the stumbling of a poor aging male adrift in a drab world. How reasonable I am to see this all so clearly, to recognize and admit my own foolishness, the emptiness of Tod's life, the rightness of returning home at night to a house where children sleep. Come what might in the morning, he had this comfort at least. He was a reasonable man and reason is what makes us human. Nodding, satisfied, he opened the bedroom door and moved on silent sock feet toward his sleeping wife, his sleeping, humorless, but not irrational wife who would not, he realized now with perfect vision, break a window in her own home even if it was a rented old schoolhouse with a belfry.

Waiting for Tom

Word traveled fast up and down Shelly Road when Trudy disappeared. There was talk of dragging the pond but nobody moved to do it. They waited for Em and Osie to ask for help, to notify police, to lead the search, but Em and Osie asked for nothing and confided in no one. Their oldest daughter had vanished, but Osie climbed into his pickup every weekday morning for work the same as usual, and Em got Jeanette and Lena off to school, then went back into her house and shut the door.

Maybe if Trudy hadn't been different from the beginning there would have been a greater stir and cry from the houses scattered up and down the road. Questions would have been asked and talk would have gone around, the sort of talk that leads to action. Instead, there was nothing more than speculation in the evening kitchens, and some wise nodding of heads over coffee.

"She sure beat a quick retreat," Angie Baraniuk said when Van came home from the mill for lunch. The four older boys were in school, but Drake and the girl, Ginnie, were at the table. "Who can blame her, coming from that snake pit. Better to be a tramp than put up with a bitch like Em—"

"Hey!" Van said, and jerked his thumb at Ginnie, who was eleven and listening hard.

"Well, they could at least pretend to look for her. It's indecent. I don't think they even went to the police."

Angie was right. They had not reported Trudy missing. Osie wanted to but Em said no, let's wait. I don't doubt she's up to some trick.

Osie didn't argue. He had given up arguing with Em about the girls—or about anything at all. In a way, it could be blamed on Trudy, this distance between him and Em. Trudy was the oldest, the first born, a boy they would call Tom. But she had turned out a girl and simple-minded to boot. Em wouldn't see it at first, and kept trying to force her into the proper mold for a little girl, but Trudy wouldn't keep her clothes on, screamed in the bath, threw toys and food on the floor, refused to talk and sometimes to hear, until Em could barely stand to be in the same house with her. It had seemed salvation when Em got pregnant again. Osie had felt the difference right away, the return of something like good cheer in the family, with Em sewing little clothes, and leaving Trudy to toddle around on her own. Osie, too, was excited. Now he would have his Tom.

But this time Tom turned out to be Jeanette. Jeanette was plump, happy, and curly-headed, and Em adored her. Two years later, she was pregnant again and this time Osie said nothing about Tom, which was just as well. The third child was Lena. After Lena, the doctor advised a hysterectomy and that was that.

When Trudy was five, Osie started taking her in the truck with him on wiring jobs and, in the evenings as he worked the garden, he told her long, slow stories about his boyhood on the farm. Trudy watched from the chair he had made from planed mill ends. She loved the stories and would ask for the same ones over and over, long after the other two girls were bored with them.

Em said, "I don't know why you bother. She can't remember from one time to the next."

But Osie knew this wasn't true because Trudy would smile when he started one of her favorites, like the one about finding his mother's wedding ring under a nesting hen after the rest of the family had given up looking. "You'd think Mom would have felt grateful to that old hen," he would say, pausing to lean on the hoe and watch Trudy's smile grow in anticipation. "But three months later that old biddy went into the stew pot like the rest." Trudy had not found this funny the first time. She had cried, but Osie explained about farm animals, and said the chicken was old and had had a good life in the henhouse. "And besides, I had to eat didn't I? To grow up strong to be your daddy."

When Trudy outgrew the stories at last, Osie worked alone in the garden, and built a bench out there from which he could watch the weather, the sheep on the low hill behind the house, the comings and goings along Shelly Road, but most of all the lively life at the Baraniuk place across the field. For two summers he watched Van and his five boys build the new house. It was a log house, big and strong, made with real logs they cut and hauled themselves. They dug the basement by hand, Van shoveling and the boys running two wheelbarrows up a ramp of planks. Osie watched Clint swing a light-weight hammer Van had bought just for the boys. He watched Arthur shovel gravel into the cement mixer, and watched Chad unload lumber from the truck. When the ridgepole was up, Osie held his breath to see Shane shimmy out on top of it to catch the ends of the rafters his dad handed up.

Osie had worked like that with his dad on the farm, had driven the team, dug the well, stood in the lee of the barn as a Nebraska hailstorm beat the young corn to death. But watching Shane on the ridgepole, he thought of the hard plywood floor far below and shook his head. He would never let his son take risks like that.

It was a bitter thought, Van with sons to spare, sons to work, sons to risk on a ridgepole, sons to pick up the scraps from the saw, sons to stand with him in the twilight admiring the day's progress. A man expected to have sons, especially a man like Osie who worked with his hands and took joy in it, who hunted and fished and wheeled his big Ford over logging roads. What sense did it make, Van with five sons and Osie with none.

Trudy was Trudy, and he loved Trudy, he realized with painful clarity as he stood in the spring garden and tried to understand that she was gone. She wasn't a son, but she was Trudy.

"She's simple-minded, Em, we have to accept that," he had said when Trudy was four. "She was born like that and there's nothing we can do about it. You can't change her."

"Change her? I'm not trying to change her. I just want her to act decent, dress decent, the way a girl should. She could if she wanted, she doesn't fool me."

A week after Trudy disappeared, Osie went to the police. The officer ran a finger up and down his jaw. "A week? A 15-year-old could be all the way across the country to New York in that time. Or dead in a ditch. Was she pretty?"

"No, you couldn't call Trudy pretty," Osie said after a deep breath. He had not thought of Trudy dead in a ditch. Em was so certain she had run off with that kid from the Texaco station who had given her a ride home when she missed the bus that he had let himself be lulled. He thought of her as she had looked last summer with her bony legs sticking out of striped shorts, her flat chest made hollow by slumping shoulders, her neck freckled, her head narrow, her hair flat and pale without being blonde. The nice thing, he told the officer, was her blue eyes, set wide and wide open from day one.

"That's the problem, I suppose. That's what worries me." Trudy was wide-eyed about the whole world, and trusted everyone whether they cared a lick about her or not, meant her harm or not. She had always had a child-like air about her that had reassured Osie because around these parts who would hurt a child? Except at school, where she was teased to tears, people generally took care of Trudy. They recognized something different about her and took her under their wing and steered her safely to where she was supposed to be and had wandered off from.

"Do you mean she's retarded?" The officer waited, pencil poised.

"No, just simple," Osie said, watching the pencil. Trudy was not smart. She had been in special classes since second grade but she wasn't entirely stupid. She liked animals and took good care of the family's four ewes and the chickens. She could cook if Em went through the recipe with her three or four times, and she could read the comics. She just didn't understand things, the way things work, or why she had to do certain things at certain times, like eating breakfast efficiently so she wouldn't miss the school bus. Osie could see her, still in diapers at three, sitting in the corner where Em had sent her for playing in her own shit. She didn't seem to hear when Em screamed that it was filthy, that she would get sick, that she would make them all sick, and why couldn't she learn to use the potty when Jeanette was already out of diapers. And then one day, they had no idea why, Trudy started using the toilet.

"She trusts people," Osie said as though arguing a point. She would talk to anybody on the street and believe anything they said. Ever since they had been old enough to talk, Jeanette and Lena had entertained themselves by lying to their sister. There were monsters in the root cellar that sucked blood. If you ate snow, you would turn white and die. They told Trudy that if she rubbed sheep manure on her chin it would grow longer and be pretty like theirs, and Osie had found Trudy out in the sheep shed, her face smeared with filth, a mirror in her hand and tears in her eyes because it hadn't worked.

"She may have made friends with someone. She had friends we didn't know about, people she talked to. Maybe she's staying with someone for a little while. She and her mother don't get along as well as they might, and sometimes Trudy gets sensitive."

"A boyfriend, you mean?" The officer's voice was matter-of-fact, but Osie flinched and thought, oddly, of Trudy and Arthur. Arthur was the oldest Baraniuk boy and, like Trudy, he was a bit strange, with one eye that looked up while the other looked straight ahead. He wasn't simple like Trudy. He was as smart as anyone but he was a softie. Or so he was called by his brothers and even Van, who had long ago given up taking his oldest boy hunting. "Arthur don't like the sight of blood," he had told Osie, and it hadn't been clear what was uppermost, pride or disdain. "He puked last time I gutted a deer in the yard. I had to get Shane to help me. Shane and Clint, they're hunters. Arthur, I don't know, I guess he'll be a vet someday. Or an old lady."

Arthur and Trudy were secret friends. Arthur knew better than to be open friends with Trudy, but when no one else was around in summer they would build little towns in the ditch out of sticks, rocks, bits of household junk, even spent rifle cartridges from out by Van's target-shooting cans, or they would weave clumsy baskets out of cattail stalks from the pond. Arthur had stopped Osie as he passed in his truck two days ago and asked if there had been any word from Trudy, his good eye fixed on Osie's face while his bad eye, unseeing, roved all over as it always did.

Arthur was a friend but not a boyfriend.

"If she thinks she can go out and live wild and come back here," Em had fumed on the second day of the disappearance, "I won't have it under my roof. There's Jeanette and Lena to think of. She made her bed, now let her lie in it."

"No boyfriend that we know of," Osie said, not looking at the officer. "She never went out. She's, um, not developed, you know."

"Doesn't matter to perverts, I'm afraid. I don't want to be too discouraging, but in my experience when they disappear at this age, they're gone, for a long time if not forever."

Another week went by. There was no word from the police even though they had put out a missing persons bulletin that went all over the country. Osie went to the Texaco station but the boy claimed to know nothing. "That kid could get lost in a hallway," he said. Osie slammed the truck into gear and sped away, and found himself on yet another long evening drive, rolling slowly along gravel roads. Looking for deer, he told Em, but his eyes were on the ditch.

Angie Baraniuk saw him go by. She was hanging out wash on the line that ran from the porch to a big jack pine in the corner of the weedy lot. "I can't understand it," she called to Van in the kitchen. "If it was my girl, I'd have the National Guard out."

"Not if she was whoring, you wouldn't"

"She'd still be my daughter." She snapped a towel out straight. "She'd get a good lickin' though."

"It wouldn't do any good to beat Trudy."

Angie had to agree with that. You couldn't hold a girl like Trudy to the same standards as other girls, girls with sense, girls like Ginnie, Jeanette, and Lena. As far as she knew, Trudy had never dated, and it was impossible to think of her as a young woman rather than a girl, although Angie had noticed a physical change toward the end of last summer, mainly a bit of swelling in the little chest. Trudy had pulled her shirt open on a warm evening and shown Angie the strap of her first bra. "It's mine," she said. Arthur, standing nearby, had turned away with a red face, and Angie, trying not to laugh, had said, "Trudy, aren't you getting kind of big to let boys see your underwear?"

Trudy had giggled and rolled her eyes.

"I saw Trudy!" Holding the screen door open and leaning in to shout, Arthur stamped the snow from his boots, stepped onto the kitchen mat, and bent to yank at frozen laces. "I saw her. She was looking out the front room window."

"No way." Angie turned from the stove, shaking her head. "I was down that way half an hour ago and I saw Em at the mailbox. She didn't say nothing about Trudy."

"It was Trudy."

"Did you talk to Jeanette or Lena on the bus?"

"They didn't go to school today."

"Well, I can't believe it. Seven months."

But it was Trudy. Before long the kids all caught sight of her standing at the window and a few times she waved to Arthur. Where she had been, and why she didn't come out of the house or return to school, remained a mystery. Bracing himself for punishment, Arthur stopped Jeanette after they got off the bus and asked how Trudy was doing. Instead of flinging the expected insult, Jeanette turned and stalked away without a word.

Angie fared no better with Em, but when she finally saw Trudy at the window, she didn't need to ask more questions.

"She's pregnant, Van. I told you so. They've got her in a big shirt but I know a baby belly when I see one."

"You ought to know," Van said. "Do you think they'll put it up for adoption?"

"No chance. Em will drown it."

Spring came late but at last the purple twigs of the willows by the pond gave way to yellow bloom and the mud shoulders along Shelly Road softened to dust. Arthur was sitting on the end of the wood pile whittling when he heard gravel crunch. It was Osie. He was striding past the end of the driveway whistling and pushing a stroller with double wheels that slid and bounced in the gravel. He stopped and waited while Arthur came up the dirt drive, pocket knife in one hand, kindling stick in the other. Osie said nothing as Arthur looked down into a pair of small bright eyes.

"She's cute," he said.

"Not she. He."

"What's his name?"

"Em favors Garret, after her dad." Osie bent over the stroller, took the blue satin corner of the blanket between two thick fingers, and tucked it behind the tiny shoulder. "We'll call him Tom, I guess. It's a good name."

"Sure," Arthur said, staring at the pink face and dark hair. "He doesn't look like Trudy."

Osie rested both hands on the bar of the stroller. "No. He doesn't look like Trudy at all." Four small wheels dug into gravel but Osie, tall and strong at 52, pushed the stroller with ease as he and Tom went on their way up the long, sunny Shelly Road.

Pearls That Were Her Eyes

Leo sits alone in the little house at Crab's Landing with night and fog outside the one big window, a good blaze in the conical fireplace, a look of quizzical reflection rather than sorrow on his face. A book is open on his lap. His feet in black socks are on the hassock, his legs crossed at the ankles. The chess table is on his left, a coffee mug of whiskey and ice on his right. He is thinking of his wife of twenty-nine years lying dead in the station wagon, and of his three children, oldest daughter Frances way off in Rome, second daughter Jessie across the continent in D.C., and only son and last-born child, Alec, just a mile away in his little student rental—all of them suffering, no doubt, but too stumped by life to begin to know what to make of the business of dying.

How like Roberta to leave them like this, barely fifty-four, no grandchildren, her daughters far away. She had been star-crossed from the beginning, had he only known it. Left an orphan at eight, raised by nuns and maiden aunts, a brief happy period as a brilliant student and then—he was the first to admit it—the Big Mistake of marrying him. How could he hold and cherish her? He had not been made to cherish anything as imperfect as a human being. No truly rational person could do this indefinitely. Over the years, he had tried to explain it to her, tried to persuade her that rational people recognize the impossibility of love, that as rational people they should pursue independent lives and friends while continuing to live together to finish raising their children. They should keep house sensibly, as though they were two reasonable men, asking nothing and suffering no disappointments.

Don't talk to me about disappointments!

Her platform rocker, on the other side of the fireplace, was empty now. Even the cat did not sit in it, but crouched on the footstool, staring, just as Leo did, at the vacant chair with the small throw rug on the seat to cover a thin patch in the upholstery. As Leo watched, the cat leaped lightly onto the chair, sniffed the rug, the arms, the back, then turned and sat facing him as though waiting for a signal or an announcement.

The bell on the front gate jangled, low and hollow.

Leo's foot twitched. Who would arrive so late and on this of all nights? Alec was not coming until morning and word could not have spread far yet. She had died only that morning. Last night she had been alive—in a coma but living—and now she lay in a body bag in the back of the station wagon.

It was possible that he was the only person in the state of California with a body in his driveway. He had not expected this. He had collected her from the hospital as soon as the call came. He had insisted on taking her away himself despite the consternation. *That's not how it's done. The funeral home. . .* He had driven directly to the mortuary but they would not take her. We don't cremate *bodies*, they said. The deceased must be in a coffin.

The deceased. His wife. Roberta.

At the lumber yard they had laughed when he said he needed the boards for a coffin for his wife who was in the car. It would be a plain coffin, a simple rectangle of clear-heart redwood, the best boards you can buy. Roberta and the redwood would go up in flames together.

Two raps at the door got him quickly to his feet which he pushed into slippers. He tightened his bathrobe belt and swung the door open.

"Was this the face that launched a thousand ships?" he boomed, as he generally did even when it was not a fisherman on the step.

"Hey, what a bum deal," Capt. Duffy said with a mournful shake of the head.

His deck hand, Ralphie, crowded in behind, also shaking his head.

"Man born of woman was born to suffer," Leo said and grasped the bottle of Jack Daniels the fisherman and closest neighbor pushed toward his hand. "Come in, come in."

"She was younger than me," Duffy said and looked at the cat in the platform rocker. "Makes you kind of think." He looked around at the two unpadded wood armchairs and Leo's reading chair, then scooped the cat up with one hand and sat down in the rocker.

Ralphie sat on the chair nearest the door, his hands limp in his lap, his face sagging with melancholy.

Leo handed them mugs, handles out. "A bit o' usquebaugh on a bitter night."

Duffy lifted his cup. "To Roberta. A fine woman."

"She wasn't happy." Settled in the armchair again, Leo addressed his socks. "She wasn't made to be happy. Born under an unlucky star."

"What was it?" Ralphie's voice, hushed and church-reverent, made Leo and Duffy look his way in surprise. Ralphie's role onshore was to follow Duffy wherever he went, to laugh at stories, to drink until he had to be steered back to his bed on the fishing boat with a hand on his back like a kid going pee at night. But not to talk. He was not a talker.

"What was it that killed her?" Leo said, musing. "Seems she must have been poisoned. A long, slow poisoning. The same poison you're drinking right now. Cheers." He lifted the mug in a salute and drank.

"Hey!" Duffy protested, but he laughed as Ralphie snatched the cup away from his own mouth and sent ice scattering over the rug.

"Cirrhosis," said Leo. "There's a lesson here. Ten years ago, she didn't drink. Twenty years ago, she was a health nut, starting every day with a cold shower and half an hour of exercise. She started drinking because life is impossible, which I couldn't argue with, but she shouldn't have stopped eating."

He had tried to tell her. *Roberta, you have to eat.* He had taken over the cooking by then and every night it was the same. He set a full plate before her and cleared the full plate away when he was finished with his meal, always putting her leavings in the refrigerator at her direction to be eaten later. Every few days, he scraped the untouched food on the accumulated plates into the garbage. If he didn't serve her a full plate, she was angry. *Trying to starve me out?* She claimed the food was greasy, that she couldn't eat it because of her gall bladder, but she said the same whether he made baked salmon, spaghetti, scrambled eggs, pork chops in gravy. He didn't like the waste.

"Cirrhosis?" Duffy's old face in the firelight was nearly inhuman from weathering, the folds and lines black with shadow. "That's liver, isn't it?"

"Liver and complications." He could tell them she choked to death on her own blood, that what she really died of, what it said on her death certificate, was esophageal varices. Varicose veins of the esophagus that ruptured and flooded her lungs. He could tell them that.

"What's the lesson?" Ralphie looked toward the refrigerator at the kitchen end of the room. "You mean you have to eat when you drink?"

"Better feed the boy," said Duffy. "You might scare him off whiskey and then what would he do for vitamins."

Standing at the counter with his back to his guests, Leo put a chunk of cheddar on a plate with Saltines, poured peanuts into a bowl, filled his cup. If Roberta were here, she would be in her chair pretending to read, her right hand raised to twist a strand of dark hair around one finger, her legs curled up under the quilted bathrobe, her glasses with the adhesive tape at one corner a little crooked on her nose, the looks she darted at Capt. Duffy and Ralphie bitter. She was right, of course. They were ignorant louts, but they were neighbors on the canal, they made him laugh, Duffy played a fair game of chess, and, by god, they lived with gusto. They lived and died with gusto. He would have more company now that she was gone. He would have to stock up on peanuts.

"The kids coming home?" Duffy cracked a peanut, tossed the kernels into his mouth, and dropped the shells on the floor.

That's what they'd done when Roberta had moved out for a year. When she returned—claiming that Leo could not survive without her, no matter what he said—she had rented an industrial vacuum cleaner on the first day. Interesting that Duffy reverted to the habit so easily. Well, as Leo had often said, a floor can only get so dirty.

"Alec's still in town," he said, "but there's no reason for the others to come back. Not from Italy and Washington, D. C. What would they do? Better to get on with their lives. They're sensible kids."

"They'll want to see her," Ralphie said with an urgency that made the two older men look at him again with interest.

"See her?" Leo prompted.

"Open casket. My mom had open casket."

"She's being cremated. She didn't believe in funerals."

"I wouldn't want to be burnt. I wouldn't burn my mother neither."

"Hell, it ain't bad," Duffy said, considering. "No worse than rotting. But I guess I'd want to see my wife one last time before."

"She'd want it," Ralphie said, a little desperate.

"She'd think it was ridiculous," Leo said with sudden irritation. What did this mindless squid of a deck hand know about his wife of twenty-nine years? But, after a silence, he glanced at Duffy and said in a low, almost coaxing, tone, "I do get to see her and so can you."

"What's the deal then, Leo? Just spill it." Duffy was wary, ready to

49

play but not yet sure of the game.

"I brought her home. She's out in the car waiting for her coffin."

The two men sprang to their feet with a shout, Ralphie scrambling away from the door as though Roberta might demand to be let in out of the night. Shaking his head, he looked with horror at Leo and then at the door and back at Leo.

Duffy recovered fast and sat down again. Watching Ralphie with delight, he said, "Me, I'd like to see a ghost in glasses. I hope you didn't leave the keys in the car, man. You wouldn't want her to go for a spin and get arrested for driving while dead." He laughed and stamped his foot. The cat shot out from under the footstool.

"Hell," snarled Ralphie. "You're sick. I never knew you were so sick. I should just go home."

"Go right ahead." Duffy canted his head toward the door that led out to the night, the driveway, the station wagon.

Retreating further from the door, Ralphie got as close to the fire as the heat allowed and stood with his back to the flames and his arms crossed.

"Pour the kid another one, Leo. How about a game to take your mind off it?"

They gathered around the chess table, Duffy in Roberta's chair that he dragged across the rug, Leo in his armchair, and, after some goading, Ralphie back in the facing chair though not before he'd hitched it a few more inches from the door. Leo stood the pair of them, a little bored with their long conferences between moves but telling himself it was better to have company on such a night, any company, than to be alone. He drank, looked into the fire, and thought, *I am bereaved.* Roberta is the dear departed. He should let people know, should submit an obituary to the *Times-Standard.* . . How Roberta would scoff. *How pitiable these lives sound, boiled down to two hundred words*, she said. *Better to bow out in silence.*

Maybe he should do another ad for public television like the one they had done last year. Linking arms on the porch of an old log house, they had danced a rustic soft shoe while singing a ditty of his creation: *Recycle old papers and twine, jam jars and containers for wine, and when I die, yes when I die, please recycle these old bones of mine.* The ad still ran now and then, popping onto the screen with no warning, making them laugh with some chagrin at just how decrepit they had managed to look, neither one yet sixty. Now maybe he should do another one by himself: *I've recycled old papers and twine, jam jars and containers for wine, and now that she's died, yes, now that's she died, I've recycled her ash on the tide.*

Roberta would love it. It might be the only thing she had loved about him for years.

"You heard about Jake and his Cadillac?" Duffy said. He was watching Ralphie, knowing the signs, the frown, the reaching for a pawn, the hesitation, the curse, the lip chewing. He was getting frustrated. He was going to blow, it was just a question of when.

"Jake Ogilvin?" Leo looked at Duffy with interest. Jake's boat, the Ginger Two was moored just down from Duffy's. Any story about Jake was a good story.

"It was last week," said Duffy. "A party over at the Vista for somebody's birthday. He got pretty lit, you know the way he does. I don't know who it was, but some halfwit joker told him Ginger had a boyfriend. He said the boyfriend watched the house and every time Jake left, he went in and planked her. First thing anybody knows, Jake's gone, driving that new Caddy. I wouldn't drive a piece of money like that in his condition,   but you know Jake. His life's a condition, if you want to look at it that way. Anyway, he saw a light in the bedroom and went crazy. He drove straight up on the lawn and smashed into the side of the house. Into the side of his own house. Damned if he didn't back up and do it again. She came out screaming but he kept smashing into the house until the car quit. Can you beat that? His own fuckin' house and car. He walked right in through the wall, no door or nothing. There wasn't anybody there. She's way past it, but you can't tell Jake that."

"Shut up. I can't think," Ralphie said. He closed on a rook, moved it, looked up at Leo's impassive face, scowled, and let the piece go.

Leo took the rook with his bishop.

With a snarl, Ralphie swept his forearm across the board. Heavy wood chessmen made a thumping shower onto the rug and rolled in all directions.

"Steady kid. Easy does it," Duffy said, and set upright again the lone knight that remained on the board. "You might end up like Jake, smashin' into your own goddamn house."

Looking at the chess pieces on the floor and at the soggy white flesh of Ralphie's back as he crawled to retrieve them, his shirt pulling up and his pants riding low, Leo wished them gone. He yawned and stretched but said nothing. He was not constituted to turn people away. *Tell them we're busy*, Roberta would plead when they heard the bell on the gate. But he couldn't do it. Who was he to shut his door against anyone who had taken the trouble to visit, especially anyone who could make him laugh. They weren't laughing much tonight, and the whiskey was about gone. They would shove off soon.

"Say, Leo. It's a real low tide out there." Duffy dragged Roberta's chair back into place and settled in it, sitting low with his legs straight out on the padded footstool. "Tide's low and you got half a dozen sand bars."

High tide, low tide. Leo admired this about his neighbors at Crab's Landing—you could wake them out of a dead sleep in a dark room and they could tell you what the tide was doing and what kind of water was running in the Potato Patch at the mouth of the bay. They didn't need tide tables. But what was Duffy up to, what did he mean about low tide and sand bars? Nobody dug clams at night.

"Hell!" Ralphie sat up and rubbed the back of his head where he had cracked it on the edge of the free-standing fireplace. "I can't reach the sonofabitch. It's way back in there."

"Never mind," Leo said. "Alec will get it tomorrow." Alec, gaunt and bearded, a reader of books rather than tides, was the only one of his three kids with Leo's taste for poetry, but why anyone would get a degree in it. . . Leo was watching Duffy. Something was up and the old fellow was full of it, being cagey, giving him sly and meaningful looks.

"Tide's low," he said again. "Sand's easy to dig. It's nature's way, Leo, you can't say it isn't. There's your boat out back."

Leo understood and wondered a bit that he felt no discomfort at such horsing around. Though, of course, it was only to goad the gullible Ralphie further. The deck hand cupped chessmen against his belly with one hand and with the other set one piece at a time on the board, each in its place.

"I'm surprised you didn't think of it yourself," Duffy said. "She always talked about the fog horn. You can't get any closer than that. Beat those bastards at the crematorium out of a dirty buck, too."

Ralphie paused and cocked his head to listen as though all that Duffy had said still sounded in the room, the syllables reaching his ears by some roundabout route, words forming and collecting in his mind like a slow train coupling. Suddenly, he guffawed.

Duffy's gaze met Leo's. Ralphie had laughed.

"Half Moon Island would be best," Duffy said, squinting and earnest now. "It's close in. We'd have the tide coming back."

Leo considered his socks. They would need boots, he would have to get out of his bathrobe, it was late and dank out there, it was probably against the law. . . such absurd laws. People had always taken care of their own, for centuries all over the world, and now this aberration of caskets and plots and bereavement counseling. What did Duffy used to call his boys when he got into a rage, before they all left home? Candy asses. The world was becoming a candy ass.

"Shit. You can't do that." Ralphie's protest ended in a giggle.

Done with the chess pieces, he scooped up peanuts and closed his hand into a fist so the nuts all cracked at once.

Considering logistics, already mentally in the boat and rowing, Leo saw Ralphie as though at a great distance. He was a speck, a drone, a rustic, a drunken fool. . . a good yeoman, salt of the earth, as worthy of settling Roberta's last remains as any pus-fingered cremationist. Oh, spare us the slick religion of death. They should have joined the Hemlock Society, meant to but didn't get around to it, a civilized end, burning without ceremony, ashes in a crock buried in woodsy ground. He could look her in the eye through that. . . her stuck, bruised eyes aimed now at the stained roof of the old Chevy, or at least in that direction through the heavy body bag.

"She in anything? A blanket or anything?" Duffy was sitting up now, hands on his big thighs, watching Leo.

"A canvas sack. From the hospital."

"One o'clock," Duffy said. "A twenty minute row on the slack tide, twenty minutes to dig, twenty minutes back, shit it's nothing, Leo. An hour and we can drink her health."

"Wi' the courage o' usquebaugh," Leo said again and stood up with the empty cup in his hand. He took it to the sink, rinsed it, set it upside down in the drainer, and opened the door. The foghorn sounded muffled tonight, distant and weary. "You'll need jackets."

"Don't you have something we could wear? If we go home, we'll miss the tide and junior here will chicken out."

"I'll find something." Leo went down the covered wooden walkway to the detached bedroom where he and Roberta had slept for twelve years, except for the time she left. The planks were cold through his thin socks. He had left his slippers by the chair. He never forgot his slippers. He could smell the low tide, the reek of the mudflats, the salty exposed seaweed, the heaviness of decomposition that Roberta swore was sewage flowing illegally into the canal.

The room was cold, damp, unwelcoming. He had lit a fire in the small stove every day during her last week at home but not once since he'd called the ambulance. A lingering taste of ashes lay on the stale air. . . *ashes to ashes, dust to dust*.

"When I was a windy boy and a bit in the black spit of the chapel fold," he declaimed into emptiness. Would she be amused to end up in a sandbar?

The lamp light was oddly dim. He snatched off the shade and tossed it onto the bed. Black shadows sprang out hard against the walls. He had built the room himself, with a Dutch double door, a round porthole-type window, and other quaint touches. But not a closet.

"Closets are bourgeois," he'd said when Roberta complained.

"So, I suppose, are clothes," she had quipped.

A rare bon mots for her but a bon mots for sure. She did have wit.

Shelves had been the solution, not tidy to look at but more practical than a closet, with everything in view and easy to find. He located boots, thick socks, a sweater and mackinaw, his old yellow tin pants, a stocking cap. He hadn't dressed like this for a long time, not since camping in the redwoods when the kids were still at home, and it always rained. Excited now, he moved fast, his hands shaking a bit as he buttoned up. The kids wouldn't like it. Could he ever explain? Their one and only mother, forever star-crossed, adrift on the sea of life, runs aground at last on Half Moon Island. He didn't have to tell them. What they didn't know wouldn't hurt. Surely it was better to believe what they wanted to believe.

A sudden softness in the knees made him sit in the only chair, Roberta's typing chair. It faced the narrow painted table where the pages of writing had grown, then vanished, then grown again, the sound of the keys forever going *pock pock pock* in the dark. She didn't need light to type. She typed what was in her mind, by touch, page after page, and put the pages away in drawers and sometimes the fire, except for the long letters she mailed to Frances and Jessie. Maybe

Frances would like to have the typewriter.

A sheet of paper had been rolled into place but remained blank. No, a single line had been typed at the top: *Ding, dong, the wicked witch is dead.*

Jesus!

He stood up, backed away, closed his eyes, took a breath, approached the table again. There were no other pages. The table was clear. She could not have meant it, not the way it sounded here, tonight, alone with her body out there. . . but she might well have meant it. She might have meant it to be exactly like this, a last joke, a last poke, a last word that meant everything and nothing at all.

The wicked witch is dead, indeed.

Snatching up an old rain jacket and Roberta's flannel-lined windbreaker, Leo strode from the room. "And death shall have no dominion!" he shouted into the black night. He threw open the door to the main room where Duffy and Ralphie waited. "Do not go gentle into that good night, rage, rage against the dying of the light."

Ralphie giggled, nervous and wheezing like an old man. Roberta hadn't minded Duffy so much, at least when he was sober. He was, she said, a man with an unschooled brain but one that picks up interesting tidbits and combines them in original ways. Which was true. Ralphie, on the other hand. . . Leo held out the jackets.

"Put the boat in the water and I'll bring Roberta down."

"You don't need help?" Duffy had one arm in the jacket. The other waved vaguely behind him in search of a sleeve. "Though she couldn't weigh much, scrawny like she was. Meaning no disrespect. I can tell you, though, I wouldn't want to pack Chardene anywhere, dead or alive. Ralphie, you shit bird, you turned it inside out. Wasn't that Roberta's jacket?"

With an oath, Ralphie flung the jacket onto to the floor.

Moving with sudden speed like a striking snake, Leo snatched the jacket up and could have sent Ralphie reeling with the back of his hand. For an instant he went rigid, jacket in hand, then folded it and placed it on the seat of Roberta's chair.

"I don't want no jacket. It ain't cold."

"It ain't but you will be." Duffy's shrug was slight. "A little cold never killed anybody yet. Anyway, you're full of the best antifreeze there is."

Their boots beat hollow on the walkway as they went around the house to the dock, Ralphie closely following Duffy. Leo opened the front gate without clanking the bell, approached the dark car, opened the hatch at the back. She was dead, dead and gone from this stiffened earthly dross that had been her bodily habitation for 54 years. Not a bad vessel for much of the time either. Slim, athletic, hair in the right places and right amounts, never turned into a cow after the babies, a matter of not a little pride to her but, honestly, he liked flesh on a woman. She had withered like an old man, nothing matriarchal about her at all, cold in the day and cold at night. She had been withdrawing from this body for years.

She lay at a diagonal, her head against the back of the front seat on the passenger's side, her feet toward the open back where he stood. Though she was in the sack he knew how she lay, and wondered how to take hold of her. He had had help putting her in, the young orderly aghast and intrigued, faces at the hospital windows above them staring. *You don't have anything to put her in*, the boy had said, tightening his grip on her legs. *The coffin's at home*, Leo had told him, lying. *The bag will do.*

And he had thought then that it would do, that he could just drive her up to the crematorium and hand her over and that would be that. But he had needed to do one thing first. Before driving away from the hospital, he had gone around to the front seat, knelt, reached into the back, unzipped the top of the bag, and pulled the sacking away from her face. Yellow skin. No glasses. Eyes so bruised they seemed to stare even though the lids were down. Hair still dark as youth but flattened and dry against the shape of her skull. Choked on her own blood but no blood around her mouth. Decent of them to clean her up.

Better they had never met. Better if she had married red-haired Bernie, unfit for the army but soon to be rich, kind as a fairy godmother, goofy with love. And then he, Leo Newlon, swaggers in from the war, muscled and brown, spouting Shakespeare like the intellectual arriviste he was. She loved cummings and he tried—anyone lived in a pretty how town, with up so floating many bells down—but he didn't really get it. They agreed on Eliot, though, and called their old farmhouse The Waste Land. She hated everything about the farm except the view. *It's cold*, she said. *Too far from town and schools. We need an indoor toilet for the kids and a washing machine for diapers. I told you we couldn't make a living off old walnut trees.*

"One of the many times you were right," he said, and leaned into the dark car to grasp her midsection, moving awkwardly in the thick clothes. She weighed a ton. She weighed nothing. She lay stiff between his curled arms. He sidled through the gate, snagged the sack and lost his balance, staggered, righted himself, and carried her up the front walk.

He had carried her across the threshold. *Oh no, Leo*, she had protested, laughing. *I'm too heavy.*

She had weighed nothing then because he was Tarzan.

She weighed nothing now because she was nothing.

Dust to dust.

The gang walk was a little tricky, with a railing on just one side, and slanted as it was with the low tide.

"Need help there?" Duffy's voice came loud from the black trough of canal.

"No," Leo growled, wanting to curse the old fool. He could carry his own wife to the boat. Feeling with his feet, hitching sideways, he descended into the stench of low tide.

He had carried her across the threshold and into the bedroom and then they had babies one two three. *I had three in diapers at one time and no washing machine*, she claimed in later years.

It wasn't true. Two in diapers, one toddling and reasonably housebroken, and the minute they moved back to town he got diaper service. For six months, as long as he could afford it. She still wasn't happy. Three babies. She should have gone to graduate school.

The babies were her life and when they left she had nothing.

An old story. She knew it herself. *An old story*, she said. *A mother with no one left to mother and too late for anything else.*

Three in diapers at once, she insisted. *And no heat but the fireplace, built of stone and big as a closet. Sucked the heat right out of the house.*

It would be cold underwater. Halfway down the gang walk, his legs shaky, Leo stopped. Below them was sloping mud, silty goo pocked with shell fragments, invisible in the dark but he knew what was there. The sandbar would be different, solid with tidy sand.

But what would Alec say? And Frances and Jessie?

"Hey, you stuck up there? Need a young buck to help you with that load?"

"Now I go forth to wander under the cold, clear eye of heaven and those weakness despising stars," he said, pitching his voice out into the fog without shouting. The gang walk rattled and he found the slanted dock with his right foot.

"Stars hell," said Ralphie. "I only wish. She's wrapped, ain't she?"

Duffy had taken the rowing seat while Ralphie hunched in the bow holding onto the dock.

Breathing hard, Leo stepped from the dock into the aluminum boat, almost lost his balance again, and sat down hard on the rear seat. He eased down the sack until it lay suspended between the gunwales.

"Kind of stiff, I guess," Duffy muttered, pulling his feet and legs away from Roberta's body. "Move her back, would you?"

Leo slid backward on the seat until he felt the stern boards press against his jacket, then pulled Roberta toward him. Ralphie shoved off and Duffy dug in the oars.

"We got a shovel from the shed," he said. "Piece of shit but at least it ain't clay out there. Why don't you get yourself a decent shovel?"

Black water gurgled, lights shifted in the fog, and Duffy's strong strokes made Leo sway on the seat. They hadn't been out on the bay much lately, with Roberta sick, but they used to do this at least once a week and sometimes would row right across to the South Jetty, or on fine days just ship the oars and drift around in the middle of the bay. Roberta would get out the thermos and two mugs, pour drinks with ice, maybe even have cheese and crackers. Gulls overhead, pelicans folding their wings and hurtling at the water like spears, fishing boats idling in from the mouth to their moorings in the canals or down at the marina by the cannery. It was a time of truce, of quiet talk, mostly about the kids. He smoked a pipe, she hunkered in the stern, always layered to comic dimensions no matter what the weather, but smiling. Travel had always been a safe time for them.

They didn't fish. They had known better than to fish. Theirs was to watch the basic workings of life, not pull the levers. This, maybe, had been the real link between them, such as there was. They were spectators at life. They went through the motions, he taught school, she had babies, they kept a household going, but they weren't of this culture and never had been. No church, no clubs, no PTA, no sports, no hobbies except books, and even, for god's sake, no TV. The ties that bind. . . it isn't enough just to watch.

His hands in his pockets, his thighs touching the bottom of the canvas sack, Leo knew that he would never tell the tale of this night. Excellent as it would be as a story, this midnight row through a tarred sea to offer up his wife to the tide, he saw that it wouldn't do to tell. It was a regrettable waste of good material but there are limits.

The boat swung into the main canal that emptied into the bay. The

60

oarlocks rattled, water dripped and splashed with the rhythm of the oars, the dark mouths of side canals slid by on the right. Porch lights glowed white rather than gold through the fog. No lights showed on the boats moored along the bank.

"Let me know if you need a spell on the oars," said Leo.

Duffy was two years older than Leo and as hard and scoured as a ship's deck. "I'm fine, going out, anyway. Tide's slack."

"Do not go gentle into that good night, rage, rage against the dying of the light," Leo said again, murmuring this time.

"We could use to have a little light ourselves," said Duffy. "I didn't think of that."

"God will light our way."

"You think so?" Ralphie's voice came faintly from the bow, serious and wistful.

"Don't make me laugh," said Duffy. "Leo never believed in God, right Leo? You're one of those whatchacallums."

"Atheist."

"Is that it?" Duffy rested for a moment on the oars as the rowboat drifted close by a dark and silent trawler moored to a dock, their wash lapping the hull.

"You don't believe in heaven?" said Ralphie. "You just die and that's it?"

"Ralphie thinks heaven is all beer and skittles from here to eternity, but I wouldn't count on it if I was him. If I was you, Ralphie, I'd pray to God there's no heaven because you sure aren't going there. If anybody went, it's her."

"Roberta?" When they'd met in the lunch line at college, Leo had fancied himself quite the freethinker, but Roberta had been far ahead of him and—most remarkable—utterly indifferent about the limits of mortality. She had shaken off her young Catholicism as clean as snow knocked off a branch. In recent years, when he joined Unitarians to find better chess players, Roberta had gone with him at first but was irritated by the ceremonial lighting of candles and the sappy songs that differed from hymns only in the substitution of words like nature and beauty for God. *If I'm going to play at ritual, I'll go whole hog for the Catholics*, she said, and stayed at home with her books. She'd be appalled to find herself in any sort of Christian heaven. Far better to wake up in the comforting heat of hell, like Sam McGee in the furnace.

"Let me off at Ole's," said Ralphie. "I'm freezing my butt. I'll walk home."

"I told you to wear that jacket." Duffy didn't slacken his stroke as Ole's dock came up, flat and empty with the Big Mama out at sea. "You won't die. If you do, we'll just make the hole bigger. This'll be good for you."

Ralphie was silent as they pulled out into the bay, the boat lifting on the slightest of swells from the mouth half a mile distant across black water. Duffy pulled harder on the left oar with each stroke, swinging them away from the bay beach. The fog had lifted some but not a light showed ahead. Duffy rowed hard, straight into nothing. In daylight, the view from here was all sky and horizon, with a sandy jetty to the west and low hills to the east, as good a prospect as any from a cemetery. Pulling the mackinaw tighter around him without taking his hands out of his pockets, Leo wished he'd brought whiskey. Dutch courage and a toast around the grave.

A score of little islands rose out of South Bay during a good minus tide, Half Moon always the biggest and best for clams. Would a clam digger uncover Roberta?

She would be long gone by clamming season.

When Jessie came home for her usual summer visit she would sit on the bay beach and think of her mother, not because she would know that Roberta was buried out here but because he would tell them that he had scattered her ashes on the bay she loved and hated. Musical water. Dank water. Brilliant water. Water as grave.

I shall wear white flannel trousers and walk upon the beach. . . Mermaids singing each to each, they always sang to Jessie, their moon child, the most contented and yet, maybe, the least fitted for life. Jessie thinks everything can be beautiful if only the lighting's right, Roberta had said once, admiring and guilty. We must have done that to her but how, two old cynics? She paints despite us. And I hope she never stops.

Jessie would set up her easel with a log for a seat and paint the bay, looking out toward the mouth where her mother's ashes had been sucked out to sea.

And on another day, Alec would sit, possibly on the same log, composing a poem about the current that had carried away the last remaining physical remains of his mother.

And Frances would walk briskly along the beach and look out at the water, the sky, the gulls, and suddenly remember that she had meant to frame the picture of Roberta cooking on a campfire. She would make a note and walk on.

"Shit!" yelped Ralphie

The boat slammed to a stop, pitching Leo into Roberta and throwing Duffy backwards onto the floorboards.

"Damn," he said, heaving to his feet. "Sorry about that. She came up faster than expected."

Duffy and Ralphie hauled the boat away from the water with Leo and Roberta still in it, metal scraping on sand. Leo stepped out onto hard footing that turned soft as he stood looking around at nothing. A smell of secret, salty life thickened the air though they'd left the fog behind near shore. They were, in truth, standing in the bay. In an hour, two hours, there would be no land here, only current and swimming things. And Roberta.

He heard the dull ring of the shovel and saw clumsy silhouettes fifteen feet away, one standing straight, the other bent. Brief irritation flared—they should have waited for him to pick the spot. But what did it matter? A sand bar is a sand bar is a sand bar. . . do not go gentle into that heavy sand.

He strode forward and took the shovel without a word. *Full fathom five thy mother lies.* The sand was hard when he slammed the blade down, but then gave, melting as though from heat. He couldn't see but he could feel the shovel stand up rigid and then go slack, and knew that it would not stand up on its own no matter how hard he drove it in. The sand that felt so solid at first impact was full of water. He had to work fast. Wishing that the others were gone, that he was alone here in this moment of powerful absurdity, he drove in the shovel, flung sand, drove it in again. He felt the hole grow but knew that the sides turned to slurry as he worked. He had thought three feet would be enough to keep her from being washed out too soon, but three feet now seemed impossibly deep. The sand would not hold.

"I can hear the tide," Duffy said and stamped his feet. "You got water in that hole. Ralphie and me had better use our hands and speed it up."

"Shit. I'm freezing. I ain't putting my hands in no ocean water."

"Then stand there and freeze." Duffy squatted and Leo could hear the scoop and slap of wet sand in between his own scooping and tossing.

"You better check the boat," Duffy said after a bit.

Ralphie slogged off. They heard the scrape of hull on sand again.

"It won't be deep," said Duffy. "Damn it's cold."

"Take the shovel."

"I'm going good here. Don't stop, it'll fill in."

They scooped and flung, the shovel splashing, Duffy cursing, Leo considering that bodies float. The foghorn sounded, deep and abiding, a companion Roberta had long known, if not loved.

"I can reach in up to my pits. It'll have to do, Leo."

"Don't stop. I'll get her."

Ralphie had remained by the boat watching the tide, and snuffled as Leo came up. Without saying a word, Leo stepped onto the slatted floorboards and lifted Roberta, his wife, the sack. This corpse, this earthly dross, this baggage, left gladly behind by a woman who had lost interest. She was gone, spared the nuisance of it all, spared arthritis, cancer, strokes, osteoporosis, incontinence, even gray hair.

Talk about Houdini. Though the weight felt like nothing, he sank deeper as he returned to the hole, and it seemed uphill as though the island had tilted under them.

"Lay her in here," Duffy said from ground level, grunting and urgent. "I'll fill it in."

Leo squatted, knees popping, sudden voices raging in his head.

"Lay her in here," Duffy commanded again.

Ralphie shouted. The tide was racing in.

Leo was standing again, clutching the clumsy burden to his chest.

"For chrissake, come on. It's now or never."

Leo stepped away from the hole and turned, looking for north. He found not a single star. "I believe she doth suffer a sea change," he said, and wished for a stool. He and Roberta would wait for the tide together. Water reached his shoes. *A sea change. . .* They would never understand. *Full fathom five their mother lies, of her bones are coral made.* A wave slapped his ankle. Boots thudded hollow on the floorboards and an oarlock clanked. The boat was there, bobbing, knocking his leg.

"Get in," Duffy said, and gripped his arm.

Oars swished and he sat down hard.

"You okay there?"

"A piece of him, sir, a piece of him." Leo slid back on the stern seat and pulled Roberta snug across his knees. She would go in the bedroom for the night. He would take a blanket and pillow to his chair and in the morning, the foggy morning, he and his son would build a good stout redwood box.

Ivan Goes Home

When I arrived at Lily's in the cold blue morning, she handed me a cup of burned coffee and said she had arranged with the social worker, George Babcock, to meet me at the Aurora Rose Café at noon. He would go with me to pick up Ivan at the foster home. Ivan's foster parents, Carl and Edith Pudleiner, had not allowed him to return to the reserve to see his mother and brother for the past six months, but this time they would not be allowed to get away with manipulating the situation.

"You make sure you don't fall for any tricks," Lily said, her breath puffing white, her arms wrapped around her shoulders in a thin sweatshirt as we stood beside the truck. "Elsie got everything ready for that little Ivan."

The Band truck was the first vehicle to travel over the smooth white road to town, newly coated with snow during the night. In no hurry, taking the curves slowly, I thought about the job ahead and tried to muster some confidence. I'd worked as an assistant to Tzeko Band Chief Lily Paul for only three months and in that time had been asked to do very little apart from simple government paperwork, delivering kids to the boarding school in town at the start of the year, helping make sense of complicated wording on official documents, and similar tasks that required very little special skill or knowledge. She'd hired me because I was there and we got along. The pay was just $300 a month but I lived free in a small log house at the edge of the reserve a bit removed from the rest of the houses. Band members supplied me with firewood and moose meat, and I was learning to fish in the lake and the Tzeko River. It was a fine adventure for a 24-year-old with no particular life plan yet.

This errand was something new and I wasn't sure what to make of it. Lily had sprung it on me after dinner, which I'd eaten with her and Patrick and the kids as I often did, the five of us making short work of the spaghetti and bread and butter. She stood up to clear the table, then sat again and said, "I want you to go to Prince George tomorrow and get that little Ivan Peter."

"She might have to kill those Pudleiners first," Patrick teased.

Ignoring him as she often did at such moments, Lily said, "Elsie was sick that time she went to hospital and Ivan got born too early. He was too little and kind of jaundiced so they kept him one month in hospital. Elsie didn't have somewhere to stay in town. She came back to Tzeko and lost her milk. We got a message for her to pick up Ivan but we didn't have a Band truck in those days and she had to take the Stage."

The Stage was a white van that belonged to a local rancher who made three trips to town each week. The passengers for the ninety-mile journey were mainly from the reserve though the occasional ranch hand with no wheels of his own also used the service.

"If we had a Band truck that little Ivan would never go to a foster home with some kind of German people," Patrick said. "For want of a truck, little Ivan was lost—what's that poem about the horseshoe?"

"Elsie didn't even get to see Ivan," Lily said. "She went to the hospital in the morning but they said to come back in the afternoon when the doctor was there. It was pretty cold out, January that time, with lots of snow."

"She went in the bar to keep warm," Patrick said, serious now.

A silence followed as though the story needed no more telling, but after a bit Lily went on. "When the bar closed she passed out on the sidewalk and almost died. They put her in jail or she would be dead today. We tried to get that little Ivan but everything bad kept happening. They sent a lady out from the courts, some kind of social worker, and they didn't tell Elsie or anybody she was coming. She just walked right into the house. Elsie got pneumonia sleeping on the sidewalk, and she was in bed, no fire, no food, no nothing. We didn't know she got so sick in the night. We found out when we went in with the welfare lady. She wrote a bad report about Elsie. I guess I would write a bad report too if I saw that mess."

The court had given Elsie the right to see Ivan for one weekend each month, but the foster family found excuses for him to miss most of the visits. In eight years he had stayed at Tzeko only about a dozen times, nearly all since he turned five. "Elsie gets ready and waits, then we get a radio message why he didn't come. She gets lonely for that little Ivan. She didn't have any more children after that, just one boy she had before, little Kenny. Ivan likes it out here, you could see he has fun with all those boys down at the lake. He likes dry meat. He's a Tzeko boy, a Carrier Indian boy. He didn't belong to any Germans!"

"You're just jealous," Patrick said, back in teasing mode again already. "You never had such a clean place as those Germans. You could eat off the floor in that house."

Lily took a bit of paper from her pocket, unfolded it, and shook it as though to clear off clinging dirt. She smoothed it flat on the table. "Listen to this piece of garbage. They got it sent by the lawyer." She read in a voice heavy with restrained rage: *Ivan has made it very clear that he prefers to be with us. When he returns from visiting his mother he is upset and misbehaves and he has bad dreams. Sometimes he wets his bed and is sadly ashamed. He is doing well now as having not visited to his mother in six months he isn't so scared. We have made papers with the lawyer to adopt Ivan and enclose them to read to Elsie Peter. We have made agreement to offer the sum of $5,000 to*

Elsie Peter for all her trouble.

"All her trouble!" Lily slapped the paper with her open hand. "What they think, she made babies for pay?"

I didn't know anything about the Pudleiners aside from the stilted words of the letter and what Lily and Patrick had said. That native children should be raised native was obvious, and Elsie Peter seemed a sweet, shy woman who cared well for her older son, but at what point does it become more destructive to change a child's universe than to let a long-ago mistake rest? Ivan had lived for most of his first eight years with his foster parents. This must count for something, possibly for a great deal, but I'd had no practice in thinking about such things and could not get past Lily's outrage and her confidence that I would return with the boy.

The road went on mile after mile, winding through dark jack pines with only the occasional opening for a rutted road leading off to some distant bush ranch. Snow had begun to fall again. Three hours after leaving Tzeko Reserve I pulled up in front of the Aurora Rose Café ready for a serious lunch and coffee. Before I could unbuckle the seatbelt, a man stepped from the covered doorway and approached the truck with such clear purpose that I rolled down the window.

"George Babcock." He offered a hand. "Remember, I'm going along to observe, not to direct the interview."

"Interview? I thought I was picking Ivan up for a home visit."

"Technically speaking, yes." Babcock's hair hung long on the neck, his unbuttoned shirt cuffs showed below his jacket sleeves, his lower lip curved over a chew of tobacco, and the hand that gripped mine looked like it had spent more time swinging an axe than filling out documents. His head retracted a bit on his neck like a turtle's and he let one eyelid drop. "What, exactly, is your connection with all this? I disremember what Lily said."

"I'm June Endersby. The Tzeko Band community development coordinator. I work with Lily."

"Right. Well, June, being new to this sort of thing, you wouldn't know how it works so I'll tell you. What you have on paper is one thing. What you have on the ground is another."

"On the ground?"

"That's right. In these kinds of situations, it's best to wait and see what comes out of the chute. They're waiting for us. Just follow me." He crossed the street, got into a blue van and set off, traveling fast.

Babcock would be no help, this was clear enough. Just keeping him in sight proved a challenge, and at one point I jumped a light to avoid losing him. He headed north toward the edge of town and turned into a new subdivision of split-level houses on curving streets. He turned again into a cul-de-sac, pulled into a driveway, and stopped with a visible jerk next to a long white car. Although there was room for another vehicle in front of the three-bay garage, I parked next to the curb at the end of a walkway that led from the street to a set of double front doors with large brass knockers. The walkway, sidewalk and driveway had already been shoveled clean of the night's snowfall but was turning white again.

As I got out of the truck one of the double doors was opened by a large, pink-faced man in a suit and tie. Carl Pudleiner did not offer his hand when Babcock introduced me but turned to lead us through the hall and into a rose-carpeted living room where Edith Pudleiner stood waiting beside a wingback chair. Large like her husband, she looked at me with tragic blue eyes. "You have come for our boy. He is there."

She pointed to a chair piled with Teddy bears. The pile shifted, and muffled, childish sobs came from inside the heap.

"I'm sorry to see everyone so upset," I said, striving for a confident and sympathetic tone. "But I'm afraid it can't be helped. Where are his things?"

The teddy bears stirred and Mrs. Pudleiner's hand flew up to her mouth.

"Who are you anyway?"

71

The question came from a young man who sat on the couch staring fiercely at me, his fists planted on his knees.

"Nine years!" Wailed Mrs. Pudleiner.

The Teddy bears heaved and several slid to the floor, exposing a pair of dark eyes that observed me with interest.

"I thought Ivan was eight," I said. "I wouldn't think an eight-year-old could fit in that chair."

Bears cascaded now, tumbling onto the carpet. A boy also slid out and stood up straight like a soldier on drill. Neatly dressed in new jeans and a button-up shirt, Ivan was a slim child whose finely-cut features and black hair could have been mistaken for Japanese. Despite the recent sobs, he didn't look as though he had been crying. He dropped to one knee and gathered the bears, snatching them up one at a time and tossing them onto the chair.

"Sit down," Carl Pudleiner said in my direction.

Babcock had already settled next to the young man, who wasn't introduced but later I learned was Ansel Pudleiner, a grown son. Babcock struck an easy pose with his legs crossed and his elbow propped comfortably on the arm of the couch. Only his jaw wagged nervously as his tongue worked at the tobacco under his lip.

I sat on the edge of the second wingback chair and considered the room. It was nothing like Lily's living room except in its striking austerity. The only evidence of family life was a set of framed photographs on the mantelpiece. The lacquered coffee table was bare, the two end tables held only a lamp with a pale cream shade, and the book shelf was empty apart from a ceramic clock, glass fruit in a bowl, and a shepherdess figurine with a flock of sheep. A gold-painted metal fan stood in front of the empty fireplace.

"Why are you taking him?" demanded Mrs. Pudleiner. "He hates it at that place. He is a sensitive boy."

Ivan stood with his hands in his pockets gazing up at the mirror above the mantelpiece, which was too high to show his reflection.

"Ivan," I said. "Do you like Elsie?"

He nodded.

"Do you like your brother Kenny?"

Another nod.

"Do you want to go to Tzeko for the weekend to stay with your mother and brother?"

Hesitating, he looked at Carl Pudleiner, then pointed at his foster mother and howled, "I don't want to go because I love her!" Mrs. Pudleiner crossed the room with swift strides and clasped his head to her flowered dress. George Babcock looked at the ceiling and chewed his snoose as though it were gum.

"You don't know what you're doing." Ansel spit the words at me. "You people don't know anything. He lived here since he was a baby. He's not an Indian any more than you are. He's decent, and clean, and nobody minds what he is, and there's no reason he should have to go out to that stink-hole they call a reserve just to make points for somebody. What do you have to do with it anyway? Why can't she come and get him herself if she's so interested. She's no mother. You call yourself a social worker—"

"It was the judge who ordered the visits to the birth mother," Babcock broke in mildly. "None of us can help that, can we?"

Mrs. Pudleiner released Ivan and sat down in the chair with the bears, pulling them into her lap. "He is such a sensitive boy," she said. "He hates dirt anywhere. If he gets up in the morning and he finds a button off his shirt he can't stand to wear it. He said the towels at that place are filthy."

As though at a signal Ivan took a feather duster from a hook near the fireplace and carefully picked up and dusted the shepherdess and her sheep, one by one.

"That's right, Ivan, Mummy was upset and forgot to dust today but you don't have to do it now."

Ivan finished the job without replying, hung the duster on its hook, and went out of the room. I had never seen a little boy spontaneously dust anything before—and I had never seen a towel at Tzeko, dirty or clean, except for the yellow towels in Lily's bathroom and the blue one she'd provided for me. I didn't know what other Band members used after their washtub baths, possibly nothing, possibly they simply stood near the woodstove until dry. Lily had warned me not to get dragged into an argument but I wasn't tough enough to be silent.

"Ivan is a Carrier Indian," I said mildly. "He needs to know his Indian mother or he won't really know who he is."

All three Pudleiners made indignant noises, and Carl Pudleiner said stiffly, "Ivan is welcome in every house in this neighborhood. Nobody treats him different, irregardless."

"We are not ashamed that he is Indian. We raised him to know about Indians. It is not their fault they are like that. Why doesn't she come and visit him here? We invited her and she never even answered."

There are undoubtedly people who can think at such moments, but I'm not one of them. With no idea what I was doing or why, possibly driven by a need to get away from this room and the people in it, I stood up and said, "I'd like to talk to Ivan alone."

Again all three Pudleiners made sounds of protest but Babcock cut them off with brisk good cheer. "That's a fine idea. I have some papers here I'd like to show you people. We'll just do that."

The sound of music guided me down the hallway to an open door. Ivan sat on his bed turning the pages of a large book about trucks, bobbing his head to a guitar tune coming from a portable player on a shelf. The room had been done entirely in blue—walls, carpet, striped bedcover, and curtains. The desk was tidy, the dresser top was bare, toy trucks were arranged on the shelves according to type and size. I thought of the double bed and patchwork quilts Ivan would share with Kenny in a room with a linoleum floor and no curtains.

"You like trucks?" I said, closing the door behind me.

Ivan nodded.

74

"Did you see the truck we'll be driving to Tzeko?"

He cocked his head and regarded me with interest.

"It's a white Chevy crew cab. Do you have a picture of a crew cab in there?"

He flipped pages quickly but with care, then held up the book to show a white pickup with bales of hay stacked in the bed. Now my feet were on the ground. I said, "I wish I had a load of hay bales on this truck. It's easier to drive with a load in back. Do you know why?"

"The wheels could dig in better," he replied as though we had been chatting comfortably for some time.

"That's right. It's called traction, but maybe you know that already. When I came into town this morning I was the first car over the road since it snowed, so it was like I was the first person who ever drove there."

"But you couldn't get lost because it's a road," he said after considering for a moment. "I wouldn't like to get lost. Explorers get lost and then they find their way out. That's why they're called explorers."

My exposure to eight-year-olds was so limited it counted as no exposure at all, yet it seemed to me that Ivan was unusually self-possessed and maybe precocious. He looked enough like Kenny that they might have had the same father, although there was no sign of a man in Elsie's life now and nothing had been said about a dad. With long hair and wearing frayed jeans he would be indistinguishable from the other boys at Tzeko. There was no sign of a packed travel bag. The Pudleiners must be very sure of themselves.

"Elsie said she has some good dry meat for you. She made it this summer."

Ivan looked pleased but said, "Mummy doesn't like dry meat. She said it makes you sick."

"So you eat it at Tzeko but not here?"

He nodded, then giggled, and was about to speak when the door opened and Mrs. Pudleiner swept in. "Well? Are you satisfied?"

"We're ready to go. Is his bag packed?"

Turning her head, she called down the hall, "Carl!"

"He doesn't need much for two days. Ivan, can you get your things ready?"

Ivan slid off the bed, reached under it, and pulled out a paper sack stuffed with clothing. He handed it to me just as Mrs. Pudleiner turned back our way. With a cry she crossed the room and engulfed him in her large arms. By the time Carl came in Ivan was sobbing again.

"We're ready," I announced, gripping the sack and moving toward the door.

"I want photographic evidence of this for Ivan's lawyer," said Mr. Pudleiner. "Don't leave until I get back."

Somehow we got out the bedroom door and up the hall, Ivan and Mrs. Pudleiner still clasped and weeping. I had picked up Ivan's jacket and boots as we left the bedroom and handed them to him when we reached the door. He pulled free of Mrs. Pudleiner to drape the jacket over his head.

"Sit down and I'll put your boots on," I said as Mr. Pudleiner slammed out the front door.

"You are the cruelest girl I ever saw," Mrs. Pudleiner said wildly. "You are killing me. Ivan, she's killing your mummy!"

"You're making this harder for everyone, especially Ivan," I said.

"I'm not taking him away—you're taking him away!"

Kneeling to help Ivan pull on the boots, I talked very low, and he stopped sobbing under his jacket to listen. "Kenny's waiting for you at the house. He wanted to come with me but Lily thought it would be better if I came by myself. He'll ride along when I bring you back on Sunday."

George Babcock and Ansel had joined us in the crowded entry hall, and soon the door opened to let in Mr. Pudleiner and a man with a video camera. "Take it all. Shoot the whole thing," said Babcock.

"Ivan," I said, on my knees and still whispering. "You're going to have to walk out of here. You're too big for me to carry and I know you can do it. It will be easier if we go fast."

With that we both stood up, he let the jacket fall away from his head, and started for the door.

"Aren't you going to kiss your mummy?" Mrs. Pudleiner pulled him to her yet again and I thought the whole scene would start over, but Ivan hugged her, wiggled free, and went out.

The drive back to Tzeko was one of the most surprising trips I was ever to make over that road. "Someday I'll have a truck like this," Ivan said as we pulled out of the driveway, and he didn't stop talking for the next three hours. Ten minutes from the house he announced that if he and I were magic we would make sure that no one in the world went hungry.

"We would have a map of the world like this," he said, and drew a square in the dust on the dashboard. "Every time somebody was hungry a blue light would go on. Oh, there it goes, Williams Lake. Zap! Now it's a green light. Everybody has lots of food." By the time we reached Tzeko we had worked our way through Canada, Germany, New York, and Africa, feeding everyone, making grass grow in deserts, and performing other generous miracles. Not once did Ivan mention the Pudleiners, or the scene we had just been through. Exhausted, unsure that I had done the right thing, I felt that our roles had been reversed, that I had become the child and Ivan was doing his best to make me feel that everything was really okay.

We pulled up in front of Elsie's house in late afternoon to find her and Kenny waiting in the open doorway despite the cold. Her face bright with joy, Elsie took the paper bag from me but her eyes were on Ivan. Kenny bounced over, picked Ivan up in his arms, and spun around in the snow until Elsie stopped him with a word in Carrier. The three of them stood looking at each other, smiling shyly.

"You want to see a movie tonight?" Elsie said after a bit. "They have some picture at the Band hall. Maybe cowboys and Indians."

Kenny said, "I wouldn't mind to be a cowboy if I didn't have to ride a cow."

Giggling, they paid no attention when I left.

The next day I returned to Elsie's for lunch, following instructions from Lily to "monitor" the situation. I should take notes, she said. "Just in case." I'd planned to take my one and only towel, washed by hand and dried overnight for the purpose, to Elsie's for Ivan to use, but in the morning I knew this was not right and left it hanging by the woodstove.

When I arrived, Ivan and Kenny were playing checkers at the wood picnic-style table that was the only furniture in the living room apart from Elsie's bed on the other side of the woodstove. Two other boys were looking on. Ivan was a checker whiz but he didn't win every game, and after each loss he leaped to his feet and did a movie-style Indian war dance, whooping around the living room to make us laugh, then returning to the game with a scowl of manly concentration.

Elsie was preparing deer meat, rice, macaroni, pickles, canned peaches, and instant iced tea without ice. Now and then she looked around the end of the dividing wall between the kitchen and living room. Standing empty-handed, she appeared amused or anxious according to how the play was going, but she never intervened, even when checkers gave way to a wrestling match that under-size Ivan flung himself into, the smaller boys piling onto Kenny.

Lunch was fast and lively, with Kenny and Ivan intent on stealing each other's macaroni while Elsie scolded, although there was no force in her voice. It seemed more than she could bear to chastise Ivan for anything. Watching him, she forgot to eat, although the rest of us cleaned up every bit of meat from the frying pan in the middle of the table. It was good meat, tender and moist, from a doe shot three days ago.

It was a good time, one of the most relaxed visits yet for me in any of the reserve houses apart from Lily's. But after lunch, hunched against the wind, I walked back to my cabin feeling perplexed and uneasy. The contrast between the Pudleiner world and Elsie's world was too great to make sense of. I had not liked Carl and Edith and their rude son but they loved Ivan, that was plain. For eight years they had raised him as their own. Winsome, precocious, lovable—they deserved plenty of credit for the way he was. Elsie loved him with anxious passion but she'd played almost no part in his daily life. *We have made agreement to offer the sum of $5,000 to Elsie Peter for all her trouble...* The sword to cut him in two was poised and ready.

It was dark by 4 now. I settled in by the stove to knit my first wool mitten and was about half done when an energetic knock was followed by the door opening. It was Lily. She rarely visited and it was not a social call this time.

"They have a party going over at Jojo Wheeler's," she said, pulling off her deer hide gloves but leaving the jacket on. "It looks like Elsie went over there. I stopped to check on that little Ivan and it's just him and Kenny sleeping. I couldn't see Elsie. I don't know who brought some booze in. I didn't see any come off the Stage."

Alcohol was forbidden on the reserve and Lily tried to be on hand when the Stage arrived to make sure no one snuck in whiskey or the sweet wine they bought in gallon jugs. She tried to be casual about it and didn't search through bags, which meant that now and again some bottles got through and then there was sure to be a party.

"We better see about Elsie," Lily said.

As usual, I asked no questions. I set aside the knitting, put on my jacket and boots, blew out the kerosene lamp, and followed Lily out into the icy night. There was enough snow now to crunch underfoot. It was vaguely luminous, enough so we could find our way without extra light. The path through the jack pines that surrounded my cabin took only minutes to walk and ended at the reserve clearing. Small, prefab houses were scattered over the open flat in no particular pattern, that is, there were no streets, just a dirt track that looped around past each front door.

The snow clouds had cleared and stars were thick overhead. Most of the houses were dark. Lily headed for the north edge of the clearing which bordered the road to town. I didn't know Jojo Wheeler as he had been working at a sawmill up in Prince Rupert since I arrived but I knew his house was the one that sat closest to the road.

We approached the house from the rear. There was no light in the small windows and I was relieved—no party after all. Elsie must be visiting one of the other houses and would soon go back to Ivan and Kenny.

"Hey," said a low male voice.

"Hey," said Lily.

The back door was open and now I could see a figure dimly silhouetted in the opening. There must be light inside after all, though very dim. As we approached there rose a low murmur of voices. If this was a party it was mighty staid. I had heard about the potential horrors of parties that got out of control, sometimes leading to stabbings, shootings, beatings, and terrible accidents. Everyone could list family members who had passed out in a snowbank and not been found until spring, or thrown kerosene on a fire to put it out thinking it was water, or slashed their leg with an axe and bled to death in the woodshed.

Lily had warned me already: *If someone asks you to keep their rifle overnight and don't give it back to them no matter what they say, don't do it.*

"I better go in there," Lily said, speaking low. "You stay here. If I have any problem you could come in."

There was no back porch. The house was set on cinder blocks and to get in Lily stepped up from the ground straight into the kitchen as though boarding a boat. She vanished from sight. Waiting a few steps from the door I smelled the usual wood smoke plus something else it took a moment to recognize. Marijuana. They were smoking dope in there. Lily had said nothing about drugs on the reserve. Straining to hear what was happening inside the house, I stood still and breathed lightly. The murmur of voices did not change apart from a short burst of laughter. A guitar started up, strummed by a heavy hand, and a flat male voice sang *I've got a never ending love for you-ou, from now on that's all I wanna do, from the first time we met I knew-ew, I'd have a never ending love for you.* Over and over again the same words.

It was too cold to keep standing in one spot so I paced, and after a bit circled the house. All the reserve houses apart from Lily's were identical government issue. Each had a large dusty picture window in the living room. Jojo's front window was dimly lit and figures were darkly silhouetted as they sat on the sill with their backs to the night. Elsie's house was up the road about a hundred yards. I was considering whether to walk in that direction and maybe look in on the boys when Jojo's front door opened. Two figures stepped out.

My quick hope that they were Lily and Elsie was over in seconds. It was two young men who jumped lightly from the porch.

"Hey," "one said in my direction.

"Hey, "I said. "Is Elsie Peter in there?"

"What's that? Elsie, you said? Who is that there?"

"June," I said. "Lily's assistant."

"I heard you was supposed to make us be good."

"Hey, I'm already good. We're all good. It's a party, hey?"

They were standing close now. The smell of wood smoke was powerful.

"I can hear singing," I said. "Who's playing the guitar?"

"Ringo. You know Ringo? That's the only song he knows."

"No way. He knows a lot of songs."

"What kind of songs? I never heard any different songs. All the time he just sings that song."

"I don't think I've met Ringo," I said, and was about to ask again whether they'd seen Elsie inside when one of them said, "We got to go. We have to go see that little Ivan."

"He hardly ever came here before. We never got to see him."

"He's asleep," I said. "He and Kenny. It would be better to see him tomorrow." Where was Lily? Where was Elsie? What was I supposed to do here?

They were moving away already along the road toward Elsie's. "We have to go back to Tatelkuz," said one. "Maybe he never would come back to Tzeko Reserve again."

"Of course he'll be back," I said, trying not to sound anxious. I should go back to the other door to wait for Lily. . . No, I should stick with the young men. They weren't drunk as far as I could tell, though possibly they were stoned. Really, they should not burst in on two sleeping boys. Kenny might be used to it but Ivan surely not, and he would tell everything to the Pudleiners.

"See you next time," one of the young men said over his shoulder.

"Wait," I called out and soon caught up with them. Side-by-side now we walked without talking, the only sound the crunch of our feet on the frozen road. My hands and face were cold. It was early winter and I had not yet got used to putting on a hat and gloves every time I went outdoors. The young men beside me were not wearing hats either. Or jackets, I noted with surprise. They wore only heavy shirts that hung loose outside their jeans, probably the checked red or blue flannel that was favored on reserve though I couldn't be sure by starlight.

We soon reached Elsie's, which was entirely dark. The young men didn't bother to knock though they did stamp their feet on the small front porch to get snow off their rubber boots. I went in last. Without having to search they located a lamp and matches. Earlier in the day the room had been loud with play and laughter. Now it was silent and blackly shadowed as we studied each other in the circle of light. The young men were in their late teens or early twenties. Both were lean, both had black hair to the shoulders, both considered me with steady dark eyes. Both wore red-check shirts though the taller of the two wore a red bandanna knotted around his throat while the other wore blue.

"Do you live upriver?" I asked.

"Tatelkuz," the tall one said, nodding and smiling. "We needed . 22 shells."

The small reserve at Tatelkuz was a two-day ride away by saddle horse. Lily had pointed it out when we were working on maps of the Band's historic fishing and hunting territories. The gravel road from town ended at Tzeko Reserve, though a rougher wagon track continued into the bush for about two hundred miles to the coast. Along it, widely separated, were a number of very small reserves, including Tatelkuz.

"That must be a long ride," I said.

"No hurry," the short one said with a shrug.

Without further talk they went up the hall to the bedroom. In it was the double bed and in the bed under a crazy quilt were the two boys, Kenny snoring with one arm flung out, Ivan on his side with his cheek on one hand and his knees drawn up. Kenny's hair was below his ears, Ivan's was cut about as short as possible without being a buzz, but they shared the same sharp little chin and the same neatly curved eyebrows.

A brief period of silent scrutiny passed. "Ivan Peter," the tall boy said, simply stating the name rather than calling it out. He turned and led the way back to the living room.

The woodstove had been damped way down and burned with low, comfortable heat. I was still a mere follower and when they stepped out into the night again I was right behind. A burst of talk in Carrier greeted us in front of the house. It was Elsie. Lily was not with her. Elsie talked quietly with the boys, talk I could not understand, and after a bit she noticed me. "You been over to that party?"

"Not inside. Were you there?"

"Me, I went to the church. Before, I didn't pray too much but I guess you have to do it sometime."

She said a few more words in Carrier and went into her house.

The three of us stood for some moments in silence before the tall young man said, "See you next time." They started up the road toward a fenced area beyond Lily's house where horses were kept, and only then did I realize they were leaving immediately for the long ride home.

Alone under the stars I walked slowly toward Jojo's house hoping to meet Lily. Far across the flat a tiny white church stood against a slope covered in dark jack pines. I couldn't see it from the road. Lily had said that on Christmas Eve and a few other days each year a priest came out from town to hold services. I had gone into the church once and gone quickly out again, fleeing the cold white room that was empty apart from a stark alter and a wall crucifix supporting the usual bloody Jesus.

Elsie had been praying in that church. She had not been at the party at all.

As it turned out, Kenny did not go with us to town on Sunday but Ivan didn't object. He was fully occupied with other matters. This time we didn't feed the hungry. We discovered giant seals that lived under the Arctic ice. We climbed the highest mountain in the world but had no trouble breathing because we could get air through our skin like frogs.

The paper grocery sack stuffed with his things sat on the seat between us. I didn't notice at first but as the cab warmed up the bag gave off a sweet smell of smoke. Elsie had taken off Ivan's crisp shirt and jeans and dressed him in Kenny's old flannel shirt and Levi's with holes in the knees. Now he was back in the town clothes and looking just as he had when I picked him up. The smoke must have permeated the bag itself.

In town, I did not go straight to the Pudleiners' though we had been told emphatically not to arrive late, definitely not after dark. We'd squeezed as much time out of the day as possible but still it was not yet twilight. I pulled into the lot of the grocery store that Lily favored. Ivan went in with me and cheerfully tossed toilet paper and packages of dry beans into the cart.

At the checkout counter I packed the supplies into cardboard boxes to protect them in the bed of the pickup, except for the toilet paper, which went into a paper sack. Back in the truck, I removed the toilet paper and transferred Ivan's things to the new bag. In the bottom, under his clothes, was a cloth bundle full of dry meat.

Dry meat was a staple on the reserve. Part of any deer or moose that was shot ended up cut into strips and simply hung from a rack in the room with the woodstove. The rising heat dried the meat and enough smoke leaked from the stoves to give a smoky flavor. The stiff, dark strings were chewy and, I'd already discovered, addictive even without seasoning of any kind. Nearly always when I stopped in at a reserve house I was offered strong boiled coffee, generally sweetened in the pot, and as much dry meat as I wanted.

Elsie had rolled the meat in a length of checked flannel that no doubt came from an old shirt. The tangy smell made me hungry, and when I unrolled the cloth Ivan grabbed a piece.

"You said you don't eat dry meat in town," I reminded him.

He chewed energetically while considering me with thoughtful eyes. "You could take it home," he said. "Don't eat it. I might get grumpy. It's mine."

"Well, you'll have to come back soon then."

He turned to look out the side window as though he hadn't heard. When, after some time, he looked back at me he was laughing. "Did you know I'm growing really fast? Faster than Kenny. Elsie said he doesn't eat his meat. I eat my meat. I always do everything. I bet I could eat three pieces of dry meat before we get home."

"You go right ahead and do that," I said, and unwound a small wad of toilet paper. "You can wipe your hands on this."

He considered the proffered paper and shook his head. "Mummy uses napkins. Elsie doesn't have any napkins. Kenny wipes on his jeans. So do I."   Very carefully, as though creating a design, he swiped his greasy palms down his skinny thighs, leaving streaks on the denim.

We sat for a while longer chewing dry moose meat that had hung for weeks near Elsie's ceiling. Then we headed for the house where you could eat off the floor.

Last Trip to the Beach

June's children sang into the dry wind that filled the car from the open windows. Her hands sweated on the steering wheel and hair from her low pony tail flicked at her cheeks as she listened, wondering that she had never noticed before how sweetly their voices blended. *This old man, he play four, he play knick-knack on my door.* . . Two boys and a girl, three, six, and eight, all brown, lean, and eager.

"I want to go to Ravioli Beach," piped Jamie.

"It's called Refugio Beach, you cuckoo clock," said Peter.

"We're not going to Refugio today," said June. "We're going to a new beach, one I found on a map. This is an adventure."

"We don't want a new beach," said Peter.

"It's a lot closer than Refugio and not so crowded. We'll be there soon."

Instead of heading south out of town as they usually did on the highway that led to a string of popular swimming beaches, June went west across farm fields on a road that soon narrowed to a lane with no shoulders. The children, of course, didn't notice the odd route. Children don't notice, not until it's too late. If she could only drive like this forever, the children held safe and singing, it would be different, it would be possible. Or a desert island. Or the stopping of time. But there are no islands, time will not stop, and the road was coming to an end. Sand grated under the tires and branches scraped the car.

"Reach me a pea!" shouted Jamie as Peter hung out the window to grab the Scotch broom.

"Don't eat it," said June. "They may be poisonous." She stopped the car and turned to look at Jamie in the seat beside her, and then at Peter and Alison in back. "You all know how much I love you?"

But they were staring out the open windows at this weird, sandy, bushy place.

"Is this a beach? I don't see any ocean."

"The road goes on a little more. We may as well drive to the end." The road did go on, but only around a few bends and then it stopped at a low dune and June saw that there was nowhere to turn around. She opened her door into a crush of Scotch broom.

Suddenly quiet, the children also squeezed out of the car. Without being asked, Peter took the picnic box, Alison the pillowcase full of swimsuits and towels, Jamie the bucket of sand toys. Lifting her heavy bag from the floor of the front seat, June thought of those silly women who carry their purses everywhere, from room to room when visiting, to the toilet, on walks, and she wondered how to explain to the children why she had suddenly become one of those nervous creatures. But they didn't notice the purse.

Sand slid and rolled underfoot, and at the top of the first low dune they stopped and stared. For as far as they could see there were hills of gray sand spotted with gray-green grasses and shrubs. The sun was hot but a cool, ocean-feeling breeze made their shirts flap.

"I can smell the beach." Peter looked eagerly about as though they had simply failed to spot the sandy shore that of course was here.

"I don't want to walk." Jamie dropped a bucket on the sand and sat hard beside it. "I like it here."

"We can't swim here," said Peter.

"I think the ocean's over there. Isn't the ocean over there, Mommy?" Alison slipped her hand into June's. "Your hand's cold, Mommy."

"My hands are often cold, little dolly." June kissed Alison's hand and released it. "Peter and I will go climb that big dune. If the ocean's too far away we'll get down in one of these nice hollows and pretend to be sand rabbits and make a great sand rabbit city and stay there forever."

"You can't build sand without water to hold it," said Peter. "We should've brought water."

It took longer than June expected to climb the sand ridge, but from its top they could see across wide and lonely distance to a shelf of blue like a mirage. Sinking to her knees, June buried her hands in hot sand and shuddered with relief and regret. Before she could succumb to the yearning to sink down full length into the earthy heat, a shout made her turn to see Jamie and Alison struggling up the slope behind them, scrambling on all fours.

"There's no ocean!" yelled Peter. And then to his mother, "I wish Dad had come. Dad can find the ocean."

"We don't need an ocean to have fun. When we went to the Oregon dunes when I was a kid we jumped off ridges like this."

"I bet I could jump." Peter bent his knees, swung his arms, and sprang into space. Whooping, he dropped into sand like flour that sucked at his feet and cascaded after him in a liquid avalanche all the way to the bottom. "Jump! Jump, Mommy. Jump down here."

They stayed on the dune for a long time, June lying on her stomach watching the kids jump and climb, jump and climb, the sun pressing into her back. Jamie got sand in his eyes and cried until June wiped it out with her shirt tail. Alison found a heavy clam shell welded into fossil and June put it in her pocket.

The sun was on the downward slope when June stood up at last and took Alison by the hand. She called to the boys to catch hold.

They jumped as one from the lip of the dune, the children landing first and letting go to tumble while June stood straight as though on a conveyor belt, riding the sand. Near the bottom, she curled, and rolled with her eyes shut until she stopped face down. The world spun in silence. If it could be like this, holding hands, a wild thrill, and then the stillness of no time at all.

No sorrow, no disappointments, no betrayals.

They drank lemonade, greedy after the dry hours on the dune, and ate sandwiches while sitting on a blue blanket. Watching her children bury their crusts, June held her sandwich but did not eat.

Alison drew a tic-tac-toe in the sand and she and her mother made X's and O's with sticks. Alison won twice and complained with a knowing look, "You let me win. I never beat Daddy."

After reading her note, he would drive out here and discover the empty car. He would call out their names, and walk up the high dune to try to spot them. He would look down into this hollow where the sun was warm and the wind was a memory and yellow broom bloomed in a circle. It was not pretty, it was too desolate to be pretty, but it was as it should be. He would be horrified, sickened, miserable, and angry. But he would understand in the end. Life, he had said often enough, is no bargain. It's not the right sort of world to have brought children into. No amount of love can protect them.

He would have to make a choice when he got here.

But how, exactly, was she to do it? Which one would be first? What if she missed? What if they looked at her, two of them, terrified and uncomprehending? And then she would turn to whoever was last—she had not thought of them looking at her, or even really being there when she pulled the trigger, but only of how it would be afterward with the four of them lying in a peaceful final row on the blanket. Could she shoot herself lying down? Would there be much blood? Surely, she was not to shoot them in the head, no, impossible.

The barrel in her mouth? What if someone stopped her before she could shoot herself and she was forced to live on without them?

Pain stabbed across the backs of her eyes. How fiercely bright it was in this bowl of pale sand. Eyes closed, she again saw Peter's face as it had looked when he came home from school on Thursday, his tender mouth tense, his wounded eyes wanting but refusing to cry. *Mrs. Geary took my scissors. She said I cut like a kindergartner. Everybody laughed.*

She had sped to the school only to find the door locked. On her way home she had stopped to buy Peter the cowboy boots he wanted from Delph's Family Shoes, and after the kids were in bed she had typed five versions of a letter to Mrs. Geary and the principal. The letters were in her purse. There was no point in sending them. The world cannot change.

"Mommy, you aren't listening to me." Jamie pulled at her arm and clutched his round brown belly. "I have to go poo."

There was no paper. June dug in the picnic box, then in her bag, her hand recoiling from cold metal. Surely there was paper, there was always paper, she never forgot paper.

"I have to go bad. I'm going in my pants."

"Wait." Picking up her swimsuit, June took his hand. "We'll wipe with this. I don't need it."

"But you won't be able to swim," said Alison.

"Don't worry, little dolly."

They squatted together behind a broom bush, Jamie with his smooth bare bottom almost touching the sand. They waited. They could not hear the wind but birds called in clear and distant voices, Peter's bucket scraped, Alison hummed a tune. It's like an island. We will stay here forever.

"Does sand like poo?" Jamie's little face was somber with thought.

"I don't think sand likes poo or anything else. It doesn't feel anything because it's not alive."

"I'm glad I'm not sand. There's an ant. I can't poo on an ant."

"Wait for it to go away. There. It's gone now."

"My poo won't come out. Something's stopping it."

"Just be patient and it will come." Hot sand pulled at June and the longing to sleep made her dizzy. Blinking, heavy-lidded, she looked at Jamie's little penis and thought that she had never really seen it before. She had cleaned it, pulling back the foreskin as the doctor had said, but had never thought of what it is, a dormant thing that would someday swell with ferocious need. . . no, it would not. It never would. It never would make a second little Jamie for her Jamie to love and, yes, to fail.

"It's coming! Mommy, it's coming!"

"What's coming?" Peter ran to them, his eyes darting about in search of what was coming, a sand crab, a giant bee, a beach rabbit, a white bird, as Jamie stood and looked down in astonishment at the great brown log he had deposited on the sand. Peter made a sound of disgust but he, too, studied what Jamie had made, and whistled.

"I did a bigger one than that. But that's pretty good for a little boy." Stooping, he picked up a stick and poked at the thing on the sand.

"Don't. That's mine." Jamie spoke so gravely that Peter stopped, looked at him, and threw the stick so that it landed with a soft sound on the sand. "I'm going to take it home and show Dad."

"You can't take poo home."

"Mommy will take it."

Caught, June gazed at her boys as though they were fresh creations on earth, beings newly unveiled, Jamie watching his turd while Peter stood over him with arms crossed on his bare chest. Boys. These were boys. Her boys. Someday, they would be men, doing what men do. Slowly, she sank down onto her heels and then all the way to the sand. She closed her eyes, shuddered, looked again at the stalwart bodies, the engrossed expressions, the tidy log of excrement that

Jamie had made.

"I'm going to get a shovel," he said with decision. "I'm going to bury that big thing."

A great breath filled June. Her eyes were wet and deep inside she felt the irresistible rising of mirth.

Not a Fair Weather Walker

During his first three months as a rooky at the *News-Telegraph*, Randy had heard reporters and editors laugh about a man who had been eaten by his pet lion in the hills south of town. He had heard them laugh about an old lady who gave away her powder-puff of a dog because her love made her feel vulnerable. (Later, anguished, she took legal action to get the dog back and lost—another good laugh.) He had heard them laugh about an ambulance that, racing back from the scene of a car wreck, had collided with a chip truck, which, in turn, had been rear-ended by an ORV and two cars.

It was no surprise, then, when they laughed about the marriage of Lyle Honeyman and Violet Trapp. "I guess it ain't over till it's over," said the sports editor. "Ask him what kind of pump he uses to get it up."

Randy chuckled obligingly. The joke was crude but it wasn't cynical. Newsroom laughter is a survival medicine, a tonic to ward off horror. And why not laugh about the marriage of two human relics, both so close to the end they've given up pretending to live like real people and taken up waiting for death in a nursing home.

"Don't call it a nursing home," the city editor had cautioned for his first real story, a break from obits and club news. "It's a retirement home. See if you can make something of it. It might be cute.

The story would not be cute. Poignant, maybe, or uplifting, or even a little bit beautiful, if he could manage it. But not cute. He was good with words and welcomed the chance to turn a potentially maudlin bit of trivia into a story that readers might remember more because of the telling than because of the facts. Make something of it? He would make a little jewel.

And wasn't there something else to be mined here, too, some uneasy fascination with the grotesque? He could feel the shadow of it as he swung off Ninth Street onto Hospital Way, which wound uphill among the dozen or so clinics and labs—each isolated by lawn—that surrounded the hospital. Who would build a retirement complex in such a spot, just a shout away from gurneys and gowns with no backs? It must be creepy for the old folks, hardly better than looking out at a funeral home. On the other hand, maybe it was reassuring. He really had no idea.

The Manor House, of cream stucco with maroon trim and balconies, rose in three stories from the hillside. The parking lot was on the uphill side, on a level with the entryway on the second floor. Pulling into one of several empty spaces, Randy sat with his hands on the steering wheel. The lot was a single strip of pavement with room for a dozen cars. A quick estimate of balconies and windows suggested at least sixty apartments, so sixty or more residents in all. If this were a hotel or regular apartment building, there would be room to park a hundred cars.

These people don't drive. These people are collected, taken to lunch, and deposited back in their cubicles.

Should he have brought flowers?

Slipping the narrow reporter's notebook into his jacket pocket, he took a conscious breath, opened the car door, and shivered. A cold wind blew on the unprotected hillside. He hurried toward the double glass doors with his head down, took the shallow steps two at a time, paused, leaned close to the glass to examine a scabbed nick on his chin, and was glad he had shaved that morning. His grandmother, dead three years now, used to nod approval when he told her about good grades and basketball triumphs, but what had made her beam was the rare sight of him in a suit and polished black shoes. That's the way a real person looks, her happy eyes said.

The door looked heavy. He grasped the handle, tugged hard, and stumbled backwards as the counter-weighted glass swung open as easily as a closet door. The door shut without a sound, enclosing him in silence, a wall-paper and silk-flower silence that reached heavy arms down carpeted passages leading off to the left and right. In front of him an open stairway curved up to a broad landing where a baby grand piano gleamed in the light of a small chandelier. Beyond the stairway small tables were scattered, empty as lily pads, and on the far side of the tables a wall of windows stood flat against gray sky.

Where were the old people?

Uneasy and claustrophobic in the thick, soundless air, puzzled by the lack of a reception desk or directory, Randy waited near the spiral stairway, but not a soul appeared and not a ripple of sound or movement disturbed the scented pool in which he remained suspended. How was he to find Violet Trapp and Lyle Honeyman?

His palms were damp. He wiped them on his jeans and felt in his jacket pocket for the notebook, a new one, the narrow pages blank except for the first one. *Violet Trapp—79. Lyle Honeyman—80. Manor House, rm 10 (not nursing home). Getting married.*

The first room down the hall to the left was 26, the numbers done in gold metal set into squares of white wood on the mauve door. Walking with firm steps, he passed glazed bulbs set in recesses in the walls alternating with art prints in gold and lavender. He reached the end of the hall. Number 10 would be downstairs, on the floor where the hill sloped away. The elevator door opened when he pressed the button and the elevator sank with such smooth silence that he didn't know it had stopped until the door slid open again. He nodded, yes, this would be easy on old folks.

Why would an old man marry? Why would an old man marry an old woman? Why would a young woman marry an old man?

Randy's high school drama teacher—gray beard, scrawny shoulders, bags under his eyes—had married one of his students two years after she graduated. Walking up the aisle, he had looked like the one who should be giving the girl away, not taking possession of her. Watching the bride with her rich red hair and carved hips under the fitted white dress, Randy had thought any man might like to marry such a woman. But what did she want? What could she possibly think she was getting? Her perfect white shape naked against the old man's deterioration. . . . old flesh in a sexual quiver—he didn't like to think of it.

Lust is not for spent bodies. An 80-yeard-old would not marry for sex.

For companionship then? But you don't have to marry for that, not when you're so old nobody cares whether you live together in sin. Or more likely without any sin at all.

Randy's mother had become a widow at 61. She had male friends, including some who had been family friends, his father's friends. What were they now to his mother? Could one of those men be more than a friend? She had survived breast cancer. He imagined her after the chemotherapy, lying gray and bony on her flowered comforter, naked, a heavy male hand on her tired skin—no, he could not see his mother naked, in fact, he could not imagine her lying in bed even with his father when he was alive. His father had been bald. Do bald men lose their pubic hair?

Jesus.

He knocked at Number 10.

The door popped open as though sprung by Randy's knock.

"Say, you got here quicker than pizza, young man. I thought it was my daughter." Lyle Honeyman stepped back with an abrupt little bow, and then, clamping Randy's hand in his, he winked a blue eye. "Don't get any ideas—she's mine."

"For heaven's sake, Lyle!" Violet Trapp, sitting among colored pillows on the far end of a white couch, laughed as she waved Randy in. "He's feeling his oats, I'm afraid." Smiling, indulgent, she pointed Randy to the armchair closest to her. "I didn't want him to call the paper but he would have his way. We have to let you men get your way on the little things so we can prevail when it matters."

"Don't you listen to her." Lyle dropped onto the couch and crossed one spare leg over the other with jaunty assurance. "You have to rule them with an iron hand, especially at first. Are you married?"

Randy shook his head. The notebook lay ready on his lap but he was unable to speak, unable to reply to Lyle, unable to join their banter or think of a question. From the silent hall he had stepped into a bright, confusing box full of good humor, flowers, photographs, colored pillows, travel magazines on a polished table. He looked at Violet. *Violet Trapp—79*. Fresh in her cotton dress, amused, intact— he dropped his gaze to the empty page.

"Will you have coffee?"

It was Violet who spoke but Lyle who popped to his feet and bustled like a young hostess to the kitchenette at the end of the room. He filled an electric kettle, opened a cupboard, took out a jar of instant, a white sugar bowl, three mugs.

"When is the wedding?" Randy managed, addressing Violet.

"Saturday."

"It would have been last week if it had been up to me," Lyle said over his shoulder.

"At the Church of the Good Samaritan. My daughter is taking care of everything."

"Were you married before?"

"Oh, heavens yes! I'm too old for new tricks." Violet laughed but not, thought Randy, with any notion of a double meaning.

"Between us we've been married one-hundred-and-two years," said Lyle. "We know what we're getting into."

"One-hundred-and-two years?" It wasn't possible.

"Fifty-three for me, forty-nine for Violet. We started young in those days, not like you kids waiting to get rich first, or become president. Our first baby slept in a bureau drawer."

"Ours had only one nightdress," said Violet. "It's one my mother made for me. I still have it."

Lyle held the small tray so that Randy could take the biggest mug. *Life Begins at 80* was written in red script below the rim.

"A birthday present. Violet had it made." Lyle sat carefully, aiming his narrow bottom for the outside edge of the cushion and then sliding back, his cup raised and steady in his right hand.

Sipping and smiling, Violet and Lyle looked at Randy. It was time for questions, real questions. . . The difficulty was not simply that these two were so far from the doddering old things of his imagination but that they seemed as though they'd been married for years already. They fit together like thick and thin, quick and slow, light and heavy. Violet full, placid, watchful. Lyle lean as grass, with eyes that dart around like a boy's, looking for something to pinch, bounce, skip across a stream.

Haven't you had enough marriage? Is love different now than it was then? Is it really love or something I don't know about yet? Randy leaned to set his coffee on the tray. "Where did you meet?"

"Here," said Violet.

"Alzheimer Acres."

"Lyle!"

Violet's cry was echoed by a meow that made them look toward the kitchenette where a black and white kitten waited outside the glass door to a tiny porch. Violet moved her foot but again Lyle was up first, saying, "Miss Lucy can't stand to be left out of anything."

"I found her on the steps two weeks ago," said Violet. "They have a rule here about pets but we haven't said anything. If you don't ask, they can't say no."

Smiling, relieved by the distraction, Randy watched the kitten march straight to Violet's foot and look up. Violet leaned, scooped the tiny creature in one hand, and held it to her face so that their noses touched. "She's the reason we're staying here after the wedding, here in my apartment. Lyle's is bigger but doesn't have the outside door."

"You won't move out? To your own place, I mean?"

"Oh, not at all. We both sold our houses, we don't need all that space anymore. It's comfortable here. And they don't mind if you're married."

"Except they charge more for rent." Lyle's indignation turned to a chuckle when Violet said, "And who insisted on paying extra to have meals sent in?"

"I like candles." Lyle winked a second time at Randy.

"Don't put that in, if you don't mind. They don't like us to use candles. They do have some silly rules."

Randy crossed out *candles*. "How long have you been single, Violet?"

"I haven't been single for fifty-one years. When you've been married forty-nine years, you're never really single again. I know that's not what you mean but it's the truth. As for the other, being a widow, Charlie's been gone two years."

"I've been alone since my Elva passed on last year." Lyle wiggled his fingers beneath the edge of a pillow and Miss Lucy pounced.

"Then you haven't known each other long?"

"Two months," said Lyle. "After Elva died, I thought at first I might as well've packed up and gone along with her. We had a good marriage, as good as any. You get used to having somebody to talk to. There wasn't anybody to talk to after. I moved over here thinking I'd meet a lot of folks in the same boat but that's a joke. I'm healthy as a horse and nobody wants to hear about that. They just want to talk about their bladder infections—organ recitals, I call it. But then I met Violet and we started going for walks, down the hill and up to Circle and back around, and we talked the miles away."

"I don't even remember what about!" Violet threw back her head and laughed.

"I started following her around. Oh, I was a regular nuisance. I liked the exercise class the best. Great views." He winked. "Some wear leotards."

"Don't put that in!"

"May I ask how old you are?" He wanted to hear it from them.

"Eighty and holding."

"Seventy-nine and feeling it."

Randy wrote the ages and traced them until they were fat. He wrote his own age, 23, next to the 80. Four score was a long time.

"Oh, I worked of course. Forty years of hard labor," Lyle volunteered. "No, really, it wasn't a bad company, we all got along. But you don't need to know that. That's ancient history, another life. I retired twenty years ago, just about the time you were born." He turned to Violet. "Of course, hers is more interesting to look back on, not being chained to a company for forty years."

"No, no, I was just a housewife. I know they don't like that word anymore. Homemaker. Is that the new one? Or maybe that's even out by now. Making a home is a job like any other, they say. But I enjoyed it too much to call it a job. I liked my home." She stroked the cat and thought for a moment. "This probably won't make sense to anybody that's never been married but, even when you love somebody, you have to let the winds of heaven blow between you. It never hurts, a little distance. After Charlie retired, I volunteered in the children's book room, but I quit after he was gone. I quit everything, even my club meetings. I didn't feel like doing a thing. As long as I stayed in that house, I knew I could never get going again. It was all still there, all the memories and life. And yet, it wasn't, not at all.

Days came and went but the memories didn't change. It was the same day over and over again. I couldn't live in a new way in the house we shared. So I left my house and came here. It wasn't easy. It was kind of like dying myself. But I must have been right." She looked at Lyle. "I came here for the social life, the bridge and dancing."

"Social life! I've seen more life in a road-kill possum. She's the only living thing in the whole damn place."

"Lyle doesn't care for bridge. I don't seem to care much about it anymore myself. We walk a lot."

"And when you're not walking?"

"Don't tempt me, young'n." Lyle chuckled and Violet set her mouth in a straight line that became a smile as she said, "He's all talk, just like Charlie, and I suppose you'll be the same someday, if you aren't already. I must be crazy getting involved with a man again— life was just getting calm and sensible." She stroked the kitten with her left hand and rested the right on the couch at her side. Lyle covered it with his, but before he did, Randy saw that Violet's fingers, unlike her smooth cheeks, were puffed like something left too long in water, the skin splotched with huge freckles.

"To give you a sensible answer," she said, "we share many interests. That's why we're never short of talk."

"What sort of interests?"

Violet's eyes, sweeping the room, fixed on Miss Lucy's glass door and the view of grass and sky beyond it. "Well, weather. We both love weather."

"Weather?"

"All weather, any weather, wind, crazy clouds. That's how we met," said Lyle. "I joined her at her table in the dining room because she was the only one sitting near the windows. It was a thunderstorm, you see, and the other old biddies were—"

"Lyle."

"They are biddies and you know it, Violet. And the men are old coots. They were all scared spitless of the lightning, but Violet was watching it crack over the valley like it was a movie. After supper, we came back here to watch some more. We aren't fair weather walkers, either."

"I suppose it seems rash to a young man that we would marry after two months. And it does seem funny when I think about it sometimes. But it doesn't seem like two months to us."

"A lifetime. I already knew Violet when I met her, if you know what I mean. It was like I found her again after a long time."

"Are you going on a honeymoon?"

"He won't tell."

"Where, you mean. It's a secret. All she has to do is pack and enjoy. I rented a car."

"What do your children think of all this?"

"You should ask them!"

"Oh, dear no," said Violet. "Going to the wedding is enough to ask. Although my daughter was all for it from the start. It was my son that was shocked. He said why couldn't we just be friends. But after he got to know Lyle, he didn't mind and now I believe he's almost as excited as we are."

"My girls don't care for it one bit. It's not that they don't like Violet. Nobody could help liking her. They're embarrassed. Plain, old-fashioned embarrassed. They think I'm a nasty old bird. They'd love to tell their mother on me. They don't know their mother. She was a good woman." He looked down at the plump hand in his and squeezed. "I suppose if I'd had a bad one the first time around, I wouldn't be in such a hurry for another one."

Back in the newsroom, Randy went straight to his desk without talking to anyone. He didn't want any other mood to interfere with his impressions. He knew it would be a good feature if he did it right, a gentle love story told with sensitivity and just the right details. There were plenty of those. He wouldn't have to exaggerate to move readers, and he didn't have to force it. He felt it. He might even go to the wedding, not to report on it—they had made clear they didn't want that—but because they had spent a pleasant afternoon together and they had urged him to come.

"Nice job," was all the city editor said, but she did not assign Randy any more obituaries and club news. During the following week he wrote stories about the one-armed pitcher on the winning city league baseball team, a lost seeing-eye dog, and a local boy who won a part in a TV docudrama. Flipping through the paper in search of the docudrama story to add to his slim clip file, he glanced at the obituaries out of habit. Something deep inside him lurched and he ducked and twisted his head, dodging the name on the page.

Violet Eleanor Trapp Honeyman.

"She died in her sleep." Lyle sat on the white couch, his hands lying still beside him and Miss Lucy, unnoticed, on his lap. "It was two days after we got back. I got up and made coffee and when I took it to her, she had her eyes open. She was happy, I know that much anyway. She loved me. Maybe not as much as she loved Charlie, but I never asked for that. What we had was different." He looked at the kitten sleeping like a rag doll in the trough between his sharp thighs. When he spoke it was low and he kept his eyes on the cat. "Sandy all but accused me of killing her mother by, well, getting her over-excited. I understand she was upset when she said it, but it's just not so. The doctor said it could have happened any time and he's surprised it wasn't sooner. She could have died on one of our walks. She liked you, you know. She was really pleased you came to the wedding. Did you see on the wall?"

Randy turned to look and there was his story, his first byline, matted and framed. *159 years to share, Octogenarians find love.*

"She said that story showed respect, something you don't see so much anymore. You know what I said? I said, 'Anybody would respect you, Violet. ' She laughed. She always laughed." He lifted a hand and set it on the kitten, and they sat thus in silence until Randy stood up to go. Lyle raised his head. "My marriage to Elva wasn't in the paper. We didn't know you were supposed to let them know. Maybe it's better to keep these things to yourself. No, I don't mean that. She was proud of it. It was nice of you to come around and I do thank you."

Randy let himself out into the muffled hall but instead of taking the elevator, he stepped out the exit door and found himself on a tiny concrete porch with dry hillside grasses growing right up to it like pale peach tidewater, gently luminous in the dusk. There was no landscaping down here out of sight of the entryway, just a narrow walk and stairs with a metal rail climbing to the parking strip. Instead of running up the stairs, Randy sat on the edge of the little porch with his feet sunk in dry grass and looked out over the town and the valley, as Lyle must be doing right now from the couch.

He sat while the valley became speckled with lights and the small evening breeze teased him with the sweet and sour smells of late summer. Sixty apartments in this place, all with people like Lyle and Violet. You could spend forever writing their life stories. But he didn't know, he really didn't know how people could go on. Would Lyle continue his rambling walks in all weather?

Standing, stretching, Randy shook his head. No, no he couldn't possibly do that. But halfway up the stairs he stopped. Of course Lyle will keep walking. He'll zip his windbreaker over a sweater, put Miss Lucy out the sliding glass door and go back inside to keep her from following, then come out the hallway exit and climb these very stairs. He won't bound up them, like me, but he'll climb with firm steps, one hand on the railing, the other in his jacket pocket—no. The other hand holding an umbrella, for the sky will be heavy with rain.

Tides Do Turn

"Say. . ." A short, red-faced man stood halfway between the checkout counter and a pyramid of 32-ounce ketchup bottles.

The checker did not look up but continued to search for the price on a package of bagel dogs a customer had brought over from Bakery.

"Say," the man repeated in the same hesitant voice. The skin of his face was thickened to a heavy grain like beach wood. His blue flannel shirt was open three buttons down, not to show off his chest like the college boys but because the buttons were gone. He leaned toward the checker with an almost yearning air, opened his mouth as though to speak, but straightened and turned away in silence to regard the mountain of ketchup.

The checker looked on the bottom of the Styrofoam package. No price there. Turning the package upright again, he frowned at the clear plastic stretched tight over a half-dozen wieners in bagel-style jackets. He looked up at the customer and considered whether it would be worthwhile to ask if he had noticed the price on the shelf. No, probably not. The customer, a tall man with narrow shoulders that drooped like warm wax, had not answered when the clerk said good morning. But there was no point in being bothered by that. In this business, you expect about one out of three not to answer your pleasantries, not to see any difference between a clerk and the computer that beeps out price readings. And no matter how cheerful and helpful you are there will always be some sourball who blames you for the price increase, for the long line on a Friday afternoon, for the brown spots on the cauliflower. This one hadn't answered even when he said, "Did you find everything?"

"Say. . ." The red-faced man spoke again and edged closer to the clerk, who heard him this time and looked around with a smile.

"Say, do you need a coupon with each of these?" The man held up a bottle of ketchup in each hand, fingers as blunt and hard as industrial tools curled around the plastic necks.

"No. No, you don't," said the checker. "You don't need any coupon at all. It's just a regular sale." He turned back to the customer who stood with his head down, looking at a newspaper on the counter. "Did you notice the price on these bagel dogs?"

The customer shook his head, his attention still on the paper.

The checker punched in $2. 29. It was just a guess, and probably too low considering the meat in the wieners, but he would make up the difference from his pocket later if he had to. It was better than charging too much or calling for a price check. The last time he had asked for a price check the next customer in line had jerked her cart around and rammed it into the express lane, smacking another customer's cart. The checker had resolved not to ask for price checks unless he had to—better to spend a bit of his own money than get customers riled up and have to endure a scene. All he wanted was to get through his daily shift as smoothly as possible so he could go back to his studies with a clear mind. It was hard enough working his way through school without having to take people seriously. The less impact the job had on his life the better.

The red-faced man was in line now, hugging bottles of ketchup to his chest.

"Thank you. Have a nice day," the checker said to the departing back of the tall customer. He expected no answer and there was none.

One, two, three, four, five, six. With respectful thumps, the man lined up six bottles on the counter.

"Wow, you must like ketchup," said the checker. If the downside of this job was having to put up with sourpusses, the upside was getting to know certain harmless oddballs who wandered in. He had never realized before how much you can tell about people by the way they shop for groceries. Like the lady yesterday, wheeling her cart up to the counter with the breathless query, "Where's your low sodium soy sauce?" Nothing odd in that until he looked in her basket and saw potato chips, frozen pepperoni pizza, fries from the deli, crackers. Of course, the soy sauce might have been for a family member on a low-salt diet but, still, he'd enjoyed a good laugh over that one.

The red-faced man nodded, serious and engaged. "I eat a lot of ketchup. You mix it with a little honey and wo'chester sauce and that's the best barbecue in the world."

The scanner beeped for the first bottle as the checker smiled at the man, encouraging and interested.

"I do a lot of barbecue," said the man. He shook his head and his voice sank to a confidential burr. "You can't lose at that price."

The clerk paused with bottle number two suspended above the scanner. "Ninety-nine cents," he said. It really was an incredible deal for 32 ounces. Six bottles was a lot of barbecue.

"You mix it with some water and add that packaged spice and you've got spaghetti sauce," said the man.

"Spaghetti," the clerk said, nodding.

The man looked back at the shining hill of ketchup. "You don't mind if I get two more?"

"Of course not. I'll just add them in." The checker restrained a laugh. Eight bottles of ketchup. What was that joke his dad used to tell about the madman and his trunkful of pancakes?

The man hurried back to the display, his step quick but solid on the glassy linoleum. A logger, thought the checker, used to making his way along deadfalls and over high creeks in the spring. No, a fisherman, with that leather face and legs that rolled to the heave of the deck. Both logging and fishing were off this year, the mill shut down, the catch hardly paying costs. They felt it even here in the store. If it weren't for the beach tourists and the community college it would be belly up for a lot of people. When he graduated the checker would not be sticking around here.

The man added two more bottles to the six on the counter and reached for the wallet clamped in his right armpit. "It's really just spiced tomato sauce. In a bottle."

Nodding, the clerk snapped open a bag.

"But you can't make it yourself at home, not like this," continued the man. "It's not the same."

"I guess they have their own recipe. If they didn't have a secret recipe, anybody could start a ketchup factory." The checker leaned down for another bag. You can't put eight bottles of ketchup in one bag unless some are upside down and they teach you that the first day—never put any container in a bag upside down. Which was funny in a way because when customers bag their own groceries they mostly shove everything in like a kid stuffing his school pack at the end of the day

"You can make pizza," the man said, his thumb in the fold of his wallet. "You take Bisquick and make a dough. You don't want to put water in the ketchup even if you don't have very much. It runs off the dough. You have to use it straight and put the cheese on top."

"I haven't tried that." The checker could not imagine using ketchup for pizza sauce, but then he wasn't any sort of cook. He lived in his own little apartment above a garage on Tidewater Drive but he still went to his mother's house every night for supper. He wouldn't have bothered with a hot meal every day on his own but it was nice to have, and it gave him an excuse to buy some of her groceries using his employee discount. And she ate better when he was there.

114

"You make chili, you can't even tell it's ketchup." The man laid out eight one-dollar bills in a fan shape on the counter. "I knew a fellow that hitched from Spokane to Florida and all the way he ate ketchup in hot water, with those crackers they have on the table. He ordered tea, in pots you know, for the hot water."

"Tea?"

"You can get refills, no charge. A dollar-fifty a meal. Not bad—until you think of thirty-two ounces for ninety-nine cents. At home you can heat your own water."

"You could pour in some creamer and it would be cream of tomato."

The man smiled, a quick, stiff smile with cracked lips. "I don't care for soup. It doesn't stick. How much longer is this sale for?"

"Two days."

"I might be back, if that's okay." The man was just the right height to wrap one arm around each sack without stooping, his wide hands grasping the brown paper as though it were canvas. With a sack on each hip, he stepped sideways to the end of the checkout stand, nodded, and turned to the door.

It was 12:45, fifteen minutes past lunch break. Looking around, the checker saw his replacement hurrying up, hands behind his back tying the royal blue apron.

The checker headed for Bakery. Those bagel dogs would make a good lunch heated in the employee microwave and he needed to check the price in any case. As he passed the ketchup he stopped, considered, took one bottle and then another. His mother used ketchup, and with his employee discount it would be another 5 percent off, though as far as he knew, she never put it on anything except hamburgers and meatloaf.

"Say."

The checker looked up and smiled at the sight of the ketchup man, who was still wearing the blue flannel shirt, though today it was wet from the rain. "Hello there."

"I don't see that ketchup. It's not all gone, is it? I just thought I'd get two more, like I said." Though he was dressed the same as before, his lips were more visibly cracked and his eyes were veined red like raw shrimp.

The checker shook his head. "It's over. It ended yesterday. I'm sorry. Maybe I wasn't clear."

The man ran his tongue over his dry bottom lip. "You said two days."

"Yes, that's right. You were here on Saturday, three days ago. This is Tuesday. The sale ended yesterday." The checker looked away, not wanting to see the man's confusion. He had lost a day somehow. And anyway, this whole pricing business made no sense, even to the checker. How could something cost 99 cents yesterday and $1. 79 today? Surely the cost of materials—tomatoes, in this case—couldn't change so much from week to week, and neither did the costs of production, shipment, storage. Naturally, the store had to earn a profit or he wouldn't be working here, earning money to finish school, but was it right to bounce the markup around so wildly? He understood the psychology of sales, he had heard it explained by the manager as well as in marketing class, and had seen it work. The store would deliberately break even or lose money on some item just to lure people in because once in the store they bought more than they'd planned to. But was this right? Was it playing fair?

The man wasn't a real sale hunter. He paid no attention to today's specials. Three cans of fruit cocktail for the price of two, and half off on frozen orange drink. He shifted in his stained sport shoes and looked at the spot where the ketchup had been but where fruit cocktail cans now made a bright tower.

"You sure it's Tuesday? I could of swore it was Monday."

"I'm sure it's Tuesday. I have Monday off. I went to the beach. It was a record low tide in the morning." The man had eight full bottles of ketchup at home, enough to last most people for years, but still the checker felt guilty as though he had somehow cheated the man out of his ketchup. And he was uneasy—the man was odd and clearly distressed. Maybe his disappointment would trigger some real trouble.

The man shook his head and blinked hard several times. "Funny. I planned to get two more bottles."

Had he been drinking? His eyes were bloodshot but the clerk could not smell booze and heaven knows, there were those who stunk plenty when they came in, the food thrown any which way into the carts—milk on top of bread, the egg carton up on end—their hands patting and reaching randomly into pockets in search of that twenty dollar bill they knew they had here somewhere, dammit. But the ketchup man was steady on his feet, his carved chin and cheeks red and clean-shaven. The shirt with the missing buttons was tucked in, and his exposed chest showed a robust pink under curling gray hair.

"Funny how easy it is to lose track of time," the checker said.

"I don't usually. I can't understand it." The man stood, waiting, as though he didn't know what to do next.

Maybe he had left a spot for the ketchup on a shelf next to the other eight bottles. The checker pictured a small white house on the road that ran along the bay, rust streaking down from rain gutters at the corners. Or a trailer out at the Sunset Mobile Park where you got to use the dock if you had your own boat. The man lived alone, a barbecue grill on his small front porch, and curled next to the porch a short-haired dog that would eat the scraps, if there were any. What did the man barbecue? Hamburger, or maybe fish from the slough, with Worcestershire sauce in the ketchup to give it bite.

It was almost the end of his shift and the checker, waiting for whatever the man would do next, looked out the window, saw that the rain had turned serious, and thought gratefully of the parka in his locker. The ketchup was still there as well, but today he would remember to take it to his mother. . ." You know, I just thought of something," he said.

The man looked up with eyes in which confusion turned to hope in an instant.

"There are two more bottles in the back. I, well, they got separated from the rest and I forgot about them. I'll be right back."

When he returned with a bottle of his mother's ketchup in each hand, the man was still standing in the same spot, his arms hanging straight at his sides, his fingers curled against his thighs. "You know, I've been thinking," he said. "I never have been a lucky person, nobody could say I have, not in jobs, or love, or easy breaks. That's just the way it's been and I haven't always accepted it the way I should, maybe, but I never gave in to it. I always kept going. And now I've got a feeling. I woke up with it this morning, the feeling that something was different. And it is different, you see? Here I miss the sale, I don't know how, thinking it was Monday but it's Tuesday and all over. What I want is two bottles. First you say the ketchup sale is all done and then you remember. There's more—two bottles, just like I came in for. That's luck, isn't it? Exactly what's left is what I came in for."

He looked at the checker, questioning, wasn't his reasoning sound? The checker punched in the price of the ketchup, the sale price, though he'd already paid for it at the employee discount price. No reason to confuse things further.

"It does seem lucky," he said as he put the ketchup in a paper bag, the small size this time since there were just two bottles.

"Tides do turn," the man said as he folded the top of the bag down. He grasped the fold like a handle. Swinging the bag off the counter, he nodded, cheerful and strong. "Have a good one."

The checker followed with his eyes as the man crossed the short stretch of linoleum, passed through the automatic doors, and headed down the walk that ran next to the front windows. His collar was turned up against the rain but he walked with a light step and the checker, watching until he was out of sight, decided that he should not feel guilty. Hadn't his sociology teacher said that perception is 90 percent of reality? Thinking your luck was turning might be enough to make it turn.

And how did he know that it had not been a matter of fate? Had anybody proved there's no such thing? Maybe he was part of the plan, maybe he only thought he was going to take that ketchup home to his mother but had set it aside by some volition other than his own just so that it would be here for the man in the blue flannel shirt. He had kept forgetting to take it home. Coincidence, fate, a random bit of luck—it was fine, whatever it was. Looking around the market, which was bright in contrast to the gray rain outside, the checker noticed a small puddle of water where the man had been standing.

Whistling, he went to get a mop.

'The wine which through the eyes we drink. . . '

Settled early in her usual seat in the center section of the small community theater, Anna Jarvis folded her hands on her program and, gazing about, felt deeply happy. She had always loved this prelude to a performance, the bustle and murmur of finding seats, the dark suits and dresses, the smiles from old friends who had been regulars at this theater for too many years to number. Mozart, Gilbert and Sullivan, Brecht, gospel choirs, children's piano recitals. They had seen it all. Some, like her, had brought their children. Those children were grown and gone now and new families she didn't know came to the theater, the kids most often in jeans and running shoes.

But not tonight. There would be no children tonight, not for a Schoenberg lecture and concert. Not for *Pierrot lunaire*.

This was modern music, difficult music, and Anna had almost stayed home herself, not wanting to suffer through jangle and discord. But she had season tickets, and she had not known quite what to expect from *Pierrot lunaire*, had never heard a "song cycle" before. She loved singing, although she knew from the write-up in the weekly entertainment supplement that this would not be normal singing, not "melodic," but nonetheless voice, wonderful human voice. The lecture portion was certain to be worthwhile, and what did she have to lose?

The university music department had turned out in force for this one, not that she knew many of them personally. She'd seen them onstage more than in the audience. There was the symphony conductor with his wife, the cellist, and just in front of them was that trumpet player who'd done such marvelous Bach last winter. The thin soprano with the bun who conducted the chamber singers had not yet found a seat and stood at the end of Anna's row gazing about with an air of elegant distance. She was joined by a tall man, a violinist, Anna thought, and as they moved forward the soprano looked sharply down and behind her.

Leaning forward slightly for a clearer view along the row, Anna saw a pink baseball cap bobbing and weaving as though to get around the couple blocking the aisle.

A child. Someone had brought a child tonight after all.

The hat darted past the soprano and moved fast down the aisle to the empty front row, turned right without pausing, and went to the center seat. The small figure turned toward the crowd and appeared to be searching for someone, though with no sign of concern.

The child was black.

Anna looked again toward the side aisle. Where the music couple had been she now saw a tall black woman standing still and composed behind two young men waiting for a white-haired woman to stand so they could get to their seats. The way cleared and the woman continued down the aisle with such a contained and unsearching air that Anna thought she could not be the mother. But, really, she must be the mother. In this small Oregon town, in this crowd, she had to be the mother.

Rather than join her daughter, the woman took a seat in the side section two rows back from the front and one seat in from the aisle. Only then did she gaze about and spot the girl, but rather than waving for her to come, she nodded and looked at her program. As though the nod had been a signal, the child spun and dropped into her chosen seat with a thud that carried above the hubbub.

You should sit with her! Anna thought with sudden vehemence. You should sit with her. You should sit with your daughter while you can. She won't stay for long. Children don't stay for long. They sit next to you for a while, one on each side like warm bookends, and then they go and your husband dies and here you are alone. *Sit beside her while you can.*

Anna aimed the thought hard toward the bent head, but the mother did not look up.

Shifting her scrutiny to the stage, she tried to see with a child's eyes and was dismayed by the stark arrangement. A black piano, a lone lectern, six metal chairs with music stands. What would a child make of *Pierrot lunaire*? Did the mother know what was coming?

The child twisted in her seat to look toward her mother, and Anna, following the look, saw that the mother was watching her daughter now. She raised her hand to beckon with that small, firm gesture that says *Come to me.* She gestured and the child stood up. Relieved, Anna smiled.

But the girl did not go to her mother. She moved one space to the left, folded her arms across her chest, and sat hard on the flipped-up seat, dropping with it, the thump sounding louder this time with the audience mostly seated and murmuring.

Heads turned. People noticed, and Anna wondered that the woman could sit so calmly, could go back to reading her program as though the girl had come to her as she had been bidden. The woman and girl might have been alone in the theater for all the notice they took of the crowd.

And yet, surely, this was admirable? To let the child be.

She never could have done it, never could have sat serenely while Toby and Karen fidgeted in the distance. She had always kept them by her. She told them about overtures and not to clap between movements, and after a while they would fall asleep with their heads on their coats, and she would close her eyes and feel the sweet music rain lightly on them, on her and her children. How lovely it had been, how rich and lovely.

But what a small window in a lifetime. Those years were gone, and what had they meant to her children? She really didn't know. Neither one had followed a music career.

How she envied this young mother! How she would love to go back and do it again, knowing this time how fleeting the time is when you have them to yourself, especially when you had just the two, so close in age. Maybe this woman had other children at home, noisy toddlers she was happy to get away from for the evening. Maybe she'd had to bring the girl, the oldest, because she was too much for the husband or babysitter to handle.

But, still, this seemed hardly the place for a pink baseball cap and such independence and restless movement. Maybe the child would go to her mother when the music started. Maybe the mother was a singer. Maybe the girl was musically gifted, but could even a precocious six-year-old get anything out of Schoenberg? Anna had taken Toby and Karen to Mozart, Bach, even Debussy, but she would have drawn the line at Schoenberg.

The girl had been sitting still, apparently staring at the unoccupied stage, but now sprang to her feet as though pricked by Anna's thoughts, the seat snapping upright behind her. She ducked out of sight. Almost instantly she appeared again and stood facing the stage while backing toward her seat. Again she sat on the upright seat but this time hung for a moment before dropping and flinging up both arms as she went down, the evening's program waving in one hand.

Anna held her breath in the sudden watching stillness. Surely the mother would take action now, would notice the disturbance and collect her child.

The woman sat on, reading her program without lifting her eyes, and suddenly Anna was glad. *Good for you*, she silently addressed the tilted head. Good for you. How silly we all are, how silly I was to keep a tight rein on my children when we were in public, as though they had no right to be what they were. . . The theater lights dimmed, voices hushed, and, sighing, Anna felt her body go light with anticipation. How she loved the peace and civility of theater. How could she have considered staying home tonight?

Applause greeted a slender man in black tails who crossed from right to center stage and smiled affably as he arranged papers on the lectern. Smaller than Anna had imagined, Martin Seidler cut a figure nonetheless, maybe because his reputation as a music historian and composer in his own right was so downplayed by his manner.

"Well, here we are," he said as though to a friend on the doorstep. "Let's hope most of us are still here an hour from now—you never know with Schoenberg."

Chuckling, at home, he appeared to be humming while he waited for the musicians in black to rustle into view behind him. A pianist, three strings, two winds, and the singer. Singer and musicians had barely settled on their chairs when Seidler, suddenly animated, launched into his lecture as though starting in the middle.

"Even now, over eighty years after its first performance, Schoenberg's *Pierrot lunaire* stuns us with its bold modernism and brilliant fusion of *fin-de-siècle* decadence, expressionist violence, and sentimentality. Few works breathe such a powerful period atmosphere and are, at the same time, so radically forward-looking."

Pleased by the confident order and intelligence of the words, Anna closed her eyes. What pleasure it was to hear talk like this, so clear, so knowing, so richly continuous with the creative past. . . "For his song cycle, Schoenberg selected twenty-one poems from the fifty rondels in *Pierrot lunaire* by the Belgian poet Albert Giraud. Through his choice and ordering of the poems, Schoenberg created a three-part tale of a creative artist's rebellion and frenzied *dereglement des sens*, the sterility and despair that follow, and, finally, the journey home.

"And certainly Baudelaire's influence is evident in much of Giraud's poetry. The spleen, grotesquerie, allegories of the poet and the world, the fascination with death and vice, entire borrowed phrases and images, have their source in *Les Fleurs du mal*."

Basking in language, Anna felt continuity as though it were tangible, as though she might touch with her hand the stuff of inspiration, ecstasy, sorrow. From Giraud, to Schoenberg, to Seidler, to her, the bright imagery lay strung across a century. Entranced, secure in her understanding of the sense of Seidler's comments if not every reference—she had not read Baudelaire—Anna closed her eyes in order to follow the words with no distraction, to run along Seidler's thought-line like a hound on a scent.

"In the first group of seven poems, Schoenberg first presents the poet reveling in the source of poetry, or moonlight, rejecting the past, then growing swiftly more disturbed. . . The most immediately striking feature of *Pierrot* is the unusual method of vocal delivery, which he called 'Sprechstimme,' or 'speech song'. *Pierrot* operates against the background of the Romantic song cycle, and the expressive force of Schoenberg's Sprechstimme in the work comes from the fact that we hear it not as heightened speech but as decaying song. The musical puzzle for vocal performers is how to determine just what Schoenberg meant by speech-song. Some singers emphasize speech over song and talk the words, and some favor melody throughout. Sandra and I believe that some words should be spoken and others pitched to hit major notes in the instrumental score. Sandra, would you please demonstrate by giving us the opening lines of 'Nacht'?"

Rising to her feet, her chest filling visibly, the soprano loosed a flow of robust German. Eerie and impassioned, the sounds slid among piano and string notes, rose above them, and then dropped to blend indistinguishably with the instruments. Despite having no knowledge of German, Anna felt that she understood nonetheless the confusion, the mystery, the pain in Giraud's *Pierrot*, and as Seidler finished the lecture portion of the program and turned to address a few low words to the players before the concert began, she opened her eyes to read the translation in her program notes, to see what lines these were that had moved her.

"Heavy, gloomy giant moths, Massacred the sun's bright rays—"

The thud of a seat flipping up was less intrusive this time, maybe because it followed sounds intense enough to have driven out a handful of audience members already. The girl was once more on her feet, a small silhouette against the stage lights. She moved yet farther down the front row to the left and sat again, this time pushing the seat down with her hands first so there was no crash. Now she was directly in front of Seidler.

The conductor raised his hand, the hall hushed, and Anna felt the familiar lift of anticipation. But a movement to her left made her look that way. The choral director with the bun was on her feet. She reached the aisle and strode down it to the second row. Resting a hand on the arm of the aisle seat, she leaned to speak to the mother.

Anna tensed as though to protest. *You can't! It's not right. . .* But she did not move. She had no right to interfere. She, too, was guilty.

In July, for a surprise holiday and birthday present, Toby had taken her on a driving trip to California to revisit spots from her childhood. The old family place in Oakland, the adobe house in Santa Barbara, the campground where she had spent summers with her parents and brother.

They had not planned a stop at Sandy Creek Beach, a favorite swimming spot north of Santa Barbara. But Toby knew the name from her stories, and when he saw the state park sign he had turned in spontaneously and eased the car down the steep entry road. The scent of a certain sticky shore plant had whisked her back sixty years. Picnics, birthdays, cookouts. Her family had been good at these, and some of the best had been at Sandy Creek .

But when they came in sight of the parking lot, her nostalgic delight had turned to dismay. Where the small gravel lot had been they found a paved and treeless flat crowded with trailers and tents, kids on bikes, families sitting around card tables set on the asphalt next to squat barbecues. They weren't terribly well off, these people, the paunchy dads, the herds of children, the towels and underwear drying on strings that sagged between a car antenna and travel trailer window.

"Christ, it's a tenement, not a campground," Toby had said.

"It's good for people to have somewhere to go," Anna had said. Her family had been plenty poor but the outdoors wasn't so crowded back then, not in the West at any rate.

And then, just as she had remembered it for sixty years, the old railroad trestle that bridged the creek canyon had come into view, its dark and intricate struts looking too frail and exposed to carry trains year after year. Could it really be the same trestle? The same one her brother had climbed to jump into the pool below as their mother pleaded caution from the sand. How high had he climbed? It had seemed a tremendous height, halfway up at least.

"I'll just step down for a quick look," she had said when Toby stopped the car at the end of the parking lot. He had followed her over white sand pitted with the tramp of bare feet, and in among towels and bodies. Veering left toward the trestle and stream, she had topped a rise of sand and looked down on a black puddle with no outlet to the sea. The glimmering trestle pool of her memory was gone.

"It's the funny weather," Toby had ventured. "The stream's about dried up."

Turning to face the sea, Anna had discovered with relief that the long line of beach to the south was as empty as it had always been.

For as far as she could see down the narrow strip of shore between the rocky bluff and white waves not a soul stirred except for three kids playing wave tag. No one wanted to trudge far through sand carrying coolers and babies.

"We could walk," Toby said, and she had almost fallen into step but then urged him to go while she would sit in the sand as she had not done for years, sit and think and remember. Alone, contented despite the disappointing changes, she enjoyed the slap and hiss of waves, the line of bobbing kelp that she could not recall having seen off this shore before, and the gentle lift and glide of gulls on a breeze that just stirred her hair. She watched the three children run from waves, shout, laugh, kick water. . . . They had done exactly that, she and her brother, hour after hour, never bored. Extraordinary how children never tire of sand and water and sun. How long had it been since she'd spent a day on the beach? Years and years. And now the bright, reflected light made her squint and long for sleep. How pleasant it would be to stretch out on warm sand and doze to the cadence of breakers.

But she couldn't lie down, not here, not fifteen feet from that big family of women and babies. Hispanics, were they? Mexican Americans. Chicanos. Latinos—it was hard to keep track of the correct term. They were very handsome, particularly the young mother in cutoffs and bikini top who sat on a rumpled red towel, a heavy braid down her back. A baby in a paper diaper crawled over her legs. Gazing out to sea, silent and aloof, she sipped from a water bottle while the others talked and laughed.

Looking down the beach, Anna saw that Toby had started back, and she watched him with pleasure, the vigorous striding figure in beige and green that was her son. She would walk to meet him.

The three kids had stopped playing in the waves and were collecting shells now, stooping to pick them up with one hand while they held their t-shirts out with the other to make a carrying pouch.

129

Smiling as she approached, Anna saw that they were picking up smooth stones rather than shells. Had they built a sand castle up the beach and needed cobblestones for the courtyard or roads? Pausing, hands in her windbreaker pockets, she watched the robust little figures, the bare feet, the rounded knees and elbows.

"Okay!" shouted the biggest boy and, as one, the three turned and fired a volley of stones at the bluff. Three gulls rose, crying, and flapped away over the water. The barrage had missed its target but the children were hopping with excitement, laughing and running up the beach.

Shocked, Anna stood still and watched them go. Why? Why would they try to hurt the gulls? She had never understood such casual violence, even as a child. But the kids had moved on to a different game now, hurling wet sand at each other. Maybe the urge to throw things, to try out their aim, was just too strong to resist. Turning away, she looked at the ocean and saw that the young woman had left her towel and baby and was standing alone not far away, watching the horizon.

Slim and straight, burnished by the low sun, she stood so long without moving that Anna thought she must be traveling far in her mind, far across the water or deep inside herself. But then she turned back toward shore and in her face there seemed to be nothing. She bent, picked up a large stone, strode up the slope past Anna, and hurled the rock at a lone gull. Striking the bluff with a crack like gun fire, the stone just missed the gull, which rose with a scream. Instead of flying away like the others, it settled again not far away. Again the young woman stooped for a stone.

Anna moved forward without thinking. Stepping between the woman and the bird, she looked into dark eyes. "Why are you throwing rocks at the seagull?"

The woman stiffened and stepped closer, so close Anna could see grains of sand strung like beads along the edge of her lower eyelid.

"People do what they do," she said, hard and furious, the hand with the stone half-raised.

Unable to move or speak, Anna stood and waited for whatever was to come next, a blow, a curse, the stone in her face.

"People do what they do," the young woman said again, her fierce eyes fixed on Anna's. She raised her arm, hurled the stone into the sand between them, and strode away.

Anna had stood where she was, paralyzed by a sense of wrong in which she was lost, unable to find her bearings, just as she sat now, frozen, watching the soprano return up the aisle with confident, even triumphant, grace. The mother remained in her seat, very still. Facing the stage, she did not look toward her daughter for several long moments, but then she turned her head as though at a sudden thought and caught the child watching her, and gestured with a hand. The little girl stood obediently and went to her mother, climbing into her lap and putting both arms around her neck as a younger child might have done. The pink cap was gone.

Seidler also raised both hands, the piano sounded, Sprechstimme vented passion into the hall. *The wine which through the eyes we drink, Flows nightly from the moon in torrents, And as a spring-tide overflows the far and distant land.*

Christmas at Charlie Creek

Until the incident with Bill Kerly's wife the night of the Christmas Party out at Charlie Creek Pumping Station, Al Shafto was known for two things—not being a talker, and the day he chased a wolf in his underwear and swore off rye whiskey forever. He quit drinking until the night of the party and there's really no question that it was because of Marlene that he went back to the bottle.

Al was different from the other mechanics and operators who worked the pipeline and who mostly came from the lower mainland or Vancouver Island. He had been born and raised up in the Peace River Country on a bush ranch that he still called home. Big, raw, and mute, Al didn't head for town on days off like the other bachelors on the pipeline. He climbed into his pickup, drove all night to the ranch, slept a few hours in the corner room that had always been his, and went out at dawn to build buck fence or cut hay off the swamp meadows with his dad or one of his three brothers.

After a break, back at the bunkhouse at Charlie Creek, he didn't have stories to tell about girls and bar fights. He listened to the others talk, laughing a little and shaking his head.

Al didn't mind being alone. The foreman, Wesley Britten, didn't hesitate to send him to one of the outlying compressor stations for a week or more. He didn't need company, everyone knew that, and he could be trusted to stay sober, to keep from blowing himself and the compressors into oblivion through an act of drunken carelessness. Even back when Al did drink, he had kept it to the long solitary evenings when the day's work was done and he was in the bunkhouse trailer frying steak and listening to the radio. This was his habit for years, until one particularly raw stretch in January when he saw a wolf and forgot everything else for just long enough to get himself into a serious fix.

He didn't have to puzzle over why it had happened. He knew it was the whiskey.

"I never would have gone after a wolf in my underwear if it wasn't for the rye," he told Bill Kerly when his solitary week was over and he was back in the coffee room at Charlie Creek. "That was a lesson I won't forget."

Bill was no particular friend of Al's but he spent a lot of time in the coffee room. It was warm in there and he got to know things. It was the only place to talk. You couldn't hear yourself think in the compressor room next to three engines with pistons as big as barrels.

Bill was short, round, and permanently red-faced under the blue cap with the earmuffs that he wore from September to June, the ear flaps up or down depending on the thermometer outside his kitchen window. As a station operator, Bill was a higher order of life on the pipeline than a mechanic like Al, but it was no secret he got there by sticking it out, by waiting until so many operators had quit and fled back south to the lower mainland that the bosses in Fort St. John got tired of bringing in new guys and promoted Bill from mechanic to operator.

Bill laughed hard when he heard that Al had damn near died in his long underwear. "I'd pay money to see that," he said.

It happened late on Al's fifth day alone out at Bubbles Substation, a five-hour drive north up the Alcan from Charlie Creek. Like other

134

substations strung along the pipeline, Bubbles was nothing more than a bunkhouse trailer sitting next to a throbbing natural gas compressor in a prefab barn. The road from the highway twisted among spruce bogs like a dropped string for about ten miles and then shot straight across a swamp meadow. Like all roads out in that country, it was mud in the spring and fall, dust in the summer, and graded snow with high banks in the winter.

Al had been doing routine maintenance on the engines, ducking in and out of the bunkhouse to warm up and wondering if he was getting old, to be feeling the cold like this. Then he looked at the thermometer and saw it had dropped to 32 below. He knocked off a little early, took a shower, and was standing in his long johns looking out the window at the twilight and drinking his third shot of rye when he saw a wolf on the road.

"When I looked out the window, I didn't see a wolf standing there," he told Bill. "I saw a new motor for Mom's well pump. A nice wolf will get you the same as a couple of beaver."

He pulled on felt-pack books, grabbed his old 30. 06, stepped out onto the porch, fired, and missed. He wasn't used to missing. He had hunted meat for the family since he was big enough to lift a 30. 30, and until he went to work for the pipeline, he'd never had a dollar to spend that wasn't made hunting and trapping.

Looking somberly at Bill, he shook his head. "I missed him. I don't know how, but I missed him. I would've tried a long shot but I saw he was trapped."

The wolf would have to run for a couple of miles to get off the road, until he came to a break in the high snow banks left by the grader. Without going back inside for a jacket or pants, Al jumped into the station truck and turned the key that was always in the ignition. He caught up with the wolf, slowed down, and was leaning out the window to take aim when he saw the road curve just ahead. He tried to stop but slid on the frozen snow, slammed into the bank, yanked the wheel, and felt the truck tip. As the truck went into a roll, he told Bill, all he could think about was the rifle bouncing around the cab with the safety off.

"I never thought I'd see the day when I'd call it lucky to get thrown out of a truck. But that was the day."

Flung from the cab, he hit the bank face first. But the snow was soft. He picked himself up, brushed off, and started walking back to the station. It was already dark enough for stars, and getting colder.

"That first mile, all I could think was hoping nobody would come along and find me in such a stupid fix. After a bit I thought I wouldn't mind if some man came along. Then I got so cold I wouldn't have cared if Miss Canada herself pulled up so long as she had the heat on."

It was the rye, he concluded. "I'd never have gone out in my long johns without the rye in me."

Bill laughed and slapped the table. He couldn't wait to tell Marlene. What was it she had said last summer? Better to keep your mouth shut and let people wonder if you're a fool than open your mouth and prove it. She had meant to compare him to big, quiet Al, he knew that well enough. Well, the dumb bush ape had talked plenty today. He'd tell her the story when he went home for lunch and then she'd see who the fool was.

"Marlene!" Bill stood in the entry hall and yelled down the basement stairs. As usual, lunch was waiting for him on the table over in the dining room. Marlene had already eaten with the boys so she could get them down for a nap before he came home, but he liked her to sit with him while he ate. And he liked tea with his lunch after all that coffee in the break room. She had to plug in the kettle.

"Marlene!"

Down in the storeroom that she had converted into a simple studio, Marlene could hear him yelling. She wiped her brush as she looked at the painting. It was nice, one of her best yet. The way the water shone like real water gave her a lovely chill. Where would she be now if she had discovered painting early, had studied it down in Victoria, not that she had the brains for college but art school wasn't exactly college, was it? She sure wouldn't be in this back of the behind of nowhere. Five houses and five trailers in a bulldozed clearing in the jack pines off the Alcan Highway. . . Anyway, she painted by instinct, not brains. She hated to leave the bright painting on her easel and go upstairs to Bill. Painting was her own, just as this room was her own even though Bill insisted on keeping his weights in here. He never used them. She had covered them with a rug. He fussed like a kid every time he found her down here.

"Marlene!"

She left the brush on the palette ready to pick up again when Bill went for his so-called cat nap. Watching him eat, she was always torn between wanting him to hurry so she could get back to painting before the boys woke up, and hoping the boys would wake up so he wouldn't make her go upstairs with him. She wouldn't be able to use the hysterectomy for an excuse much longer. But at least there would be no more pregnancies. At least not that. She would be her old slim self again by Christmas. She would wear the blue dress to the party.

It was the supervisor, Wes Britten, and his wife, Karen, who gave the Christmas party every year at Charlie Creek Station. Wes and Karen lived in the house next to Bill and Marlene's.

"You have to have the party," Marlene had insisted to Karen when she said she was sick of it. "Wes is the boss. And I'm making a new dress."

"Why don't we just show the video of last year's party and call it done?" Karen had said, curling her lip with conscious ugliness. "It's the same party every year anyway."

Brenda Pool would get smashed and be halfway into a striptease before it hit Skip that it was his own wife that everybody—including him—was cheering on to the finish. He and Karen had practically had to tie her up in her coat last year to get her out the door. And Bill would throw up. Last year he would have made it to the toilet on time except that the door, mysteriously, was locked with no one inside. Karen had told Marlene she suspected one of the casuals of locking it on purpose, the redheaded kid from Prince George most likely.

"I don't blame him," she said. "At least he got some fun out of the evening."

"I'll help you decorate," Marlene had offered. She helped every year.

"One good thing anyway. We don't have to wonder if anyone will come to the party," Karen had said without humor.

They all came to the Christmas party that year, even Al Shafto who never partied. And, as usual, they stood around for the first hour like wax dummies, as though they hardly knew each other, as though they didn't see each other every day of the year. Brenda Pool was strapless, and Marlene was an angel in baby blue as she stood in the doorway of the basement rec room and gazed around like an eager child.

"You look darling," Karen said, and patted Marlene's hand as she edged past her to collect Wes from upstairs. He was in the spare bedroom they called the study, drinking, playing the expansive host and pouring freely, mainly into his own glass.

Marlene grabbed Karen's arm and squeezed before letting her go. Excited and oddly nervous, she let her eyes run around the room, taking in Brenda's bare shoulders and Lily Bruneau's old-fashioned lace collar that lay on her explosive bosom like doilies on two chair arms. Karen was in black, like last year. Black for Christmas? Well, blue wasn't Christmasy either. , "What do you think it is, Easter?" Bill had snorted when Marlene came out of the bathroom after drying her long hair, and he hadn't appeared to notice that she looked wonderful—better than she ever had before, even she could see that.

I look like an angel, thought Marlene, her eyes searching the dim room. Pure, blonde, blue, floating. She had never looked better, not in high school, when her skin was blotchy, and not in the years after she married, when she was always chalky with morning sickness or purple-eyed from getting up with the boys. But those days were forever gone, thanks to the hysterectomy. Her skin, for the first time ever, was smooth and even in color. Bullied by the doctor down in Fort St. John, she had started to exercise after the operation, peddling ten miles every day on Bill's workout bike, which he never used after making such a fuss about ordering the model with the odometer. When it was nice out, she pulled Sammy on the sled, up and down the icy sidewalk past the five houses and five trailers, around almost to the pumping station, out to the highway, tilting her head back to the sky when no one was looking. A little sun, even in winter. A little pink in the cheeks. Pink and blue.

But where was Al? He had said he would be here.

Al was upstairs drinking with Wes, Bill, and Skip Pool. Even though it was known that he had quit drinking after the wolf incident, Al was an easy target for Wes's jovial arm as he stood, uncertain, just inside the door.

"I never drink unless I'm alone or with somebody," Wes said, pressing a water glass of whiskey into his hand with a wink.

"I'm countin' the days," said Pool, tilting his head to keep the cigarette smoke out of his eyes. He and Bill were heading down for a week of training in Prince George after the first of the year.

"You taking Brenda?" Bill reached for his sixth beer.

"Are you kiddin'? That's like taking a sandwich to a banquet!"

The men laughed. A sandwich to a banquet. A good one, a really good one.

The door opened and Karen came in. "Hi, Al," she said, openly surprised but in the next moment trying to cover it. "Glad you could make it with the snow and everything." She took her husband's arm.

"If we get it started, people will dance."

For a long moment, Wes didn't move. He looked at the two men on the brown leatherette couch and at Al leaning into the wall. With a growl, he said, "Let's see if you turkeys can dance."

The others followed the couple out. Al, going last, tipped the bottle of rye into his mouth and held it there until it was empty. He took a powerful breath and smiled. He reached the party room just behind Bill and Skip but held back when they dived into the crowd and headed for the drinks table. Scanning the room over the heads of the dancers who had stood up as soon as Wes and Karen took the floor, he fixed on a blue dress. Blue eyes returned his look. He turned away and found himself face to face with Brenda Pool and her white shoulders and laughing red mouth. She touched the front of his white shirt with fingers that flashed red at the tips.

Al backed away and ducked under a swag of crepe paper.

The room seethed. Claude and Lily Bruneau gyrated like teenagers, Donny Babcock swung his mother-in-law who was up from Kelowna for Christmas, women's faces shone pink under the paper lanterns, men grinned as they danced with a touch of stiffness in the shoulders.

Sidling around the bobbing crowd, Marlene was headed for the soft drink tub when one of the casuals tapped her shoulder. She had seen him around the bunkhouse a few times since fall and knew he was just up from the lower mainland, a flunky to the mechanics. But he was blonde and blue-eyed like her, and movie-perfect like some of the boys she had wanted in high school but who never gave her a look. She held her head up. She was right. She did look good tonight, she could tell by the boy's eyes. Not touching, they stepped out onto the floor just as the music stopped.

"The next one then," the boy said. "You're Marlene. My name's Lanny."

"I know."

The next one was a slow dance and Marlene was dismayed to see that only Brenda and Skip had stayed on the floor. Ah, thank god, Wes was pulling Lily from her chair. Marlene looked at Lanny, felt his hand settle on her waist, raised her hand to his shoulder, and turned her head so that her cheek did not quite touch his shirt. Her hair was warm fur against her own neck and shoulders and the hand on her waist was confident. She was going to enjoy herself tonight no matter what.

And then Lanny stopped even though the music continued, and Marlene saw Bill's red face where Lanny's shoulder had been. Confused, she looked at the young man, saw him shrug and felt cool air on her palm as he released her hand. Bill clamped his arm around her, pinning her to his soft belly. Not a word passed between them until the dance was done, when he steered her to an empty chair.

"Sit here before you fall down and make a fool of the both of us," he said, low but distinct, as though she might already be too far gone to grasp his meaning.

Fall down? Fall down! She had been drinking straight Coke. The party had barely started, and it was Bill who stank of beer already. She stayed by the chair until she saw Bill in a huddle with Skip and Donny. Working her way around the dancers, she found Karen at the drinks table pouring gin into a beer mug half full of Seven-Up.

"Build yourself a happy, kid," she said. "Come to think of it, are you old enough to drink, Miss Prom Queen?"

Marlene had to laugh. If only it were true. "I'll trade you a diamond for a rum and Coke," she said, tugging at her wedding ring.

"Done. But keep the ring. It would just fall off my bony fingers into the dishwater. Anyway, you might need to sell it sometime." Karen poured Coke into a 16-ounce paper cup and sloshed in rum until Marlene grabbed her thin wrist with a cry.

"What are you, a woman or a mouse?" Karen filled the cup and stirred the drink with a plastic fork.

Marlene took the drink in her left hand and with her right she took Karen's other hand and squeezed it once, hard, and then giggled. Last week, she and Karen had taken the Skidoos out for a run and stopped at an overlook so Karen could have a smoke. Noticing a yellow pee hole in the snow, Karen had dropped to her knees, sniffed at the pee, and grunted, "Skip Pool. Yesterday. Three o'clock."

What a character. How much stupider Charlie Creek Station would be without Karen. Should she ask her about Al? What do you think of Al? Do you ever wonder why Al isn't married? Did you know Al told me all about the wolf chase and it wasn't like Bill said at all. . . She couldn't talk to Karen about Al. Karen would say, *You like him? Go for him!* As though it could be that easy. And as if Karen would ever do such a thing herself. The way she stood by Wes was a wonder. She hated Charlie Creek as much as Marlene did but she never blamed Wes for it, for losing their breezy ranch-style house down in the Okanagan and getting transferred up here to Siberia—a promotion, they called it, but everybody knew it was because of the booze. Exile.

Wes drank. Skip drank. Bill drank. Everybody drank in this frozen hell hole. Except Al, at least since the wolf chase. Marlene tipped the big cup and swallowed with her eyes closed. Just a kid getting down a pill.

Al, leaning against the wall, had watched Marlene dance with Lanny and then Bill. He had watched Bill steer her to a chair and leave her standing with a fixed look. He watched her circle to the table where she stood with Karen Britten, her little back toward him, her shoulder blades distinct under the blue cloth. Where had she found that dress the same blue as her eyes? Dancers came between them, washed away, came between them. When the floor cleared during a break in the music, she was gone.

"Lose your huntin' dog?" Claude Bruneau grinned up at Al, his eyes bright, nose red, belly hanging out over his belt like a Christmas pillow wrapped in his candy-stripe shirt. "What I'm waitin' for is

Brenda to cut loose," he said. "Bill's doin' his best to get her drunk—only she don't have so much to take off this year!" He threw his head back and roared.

"What's the joke, boys?" Lily said, coming up behind her husband and taking him by the arm. "Come on, Claude. Or should I dance with Al?"

"Al don't want to dance with an old married lady like you. He's got other fish to fry." Claude's wink was so weighty it might have toppled him except that Lily had him by the arm. She led him away.

Al moved ever so gradually toward the bright rectangle of door that led to the hall, the stairs, the front entry, the cool night. He didn't know why he'd driven so far for a party, all the talk and noise, everybody acting different just because it was a party. After being dry for so long he felt like a twister had slipped into his head on the heels of the rye. He wouldn't have minded a dance with Marlene, she had been so sweet to him that day he had to wait for Bill at the house. They just sat there in the twilight—she hadn't turned on any lights until they heard Bill's truck—and talked. She had asked him about the wolf chase and he had flamed with embarrassment, not knowing how to talk to a woman about walking around in his underwear. But she hadn't seemed to notice his red face in the dimness. She sat forward, so serious and interested that he told her the whole story, even the part about not wanting anybody to come along and find him.

She had laughed at that, knowingly, as though they shared a secret. "You must be tough," she said. "I would've died in the first mile."

No, he had said, shaking his head. I was just lucky I didn't drive too far to walk back before I froze. Or get shot when that gun started flying around. I never was colder in my life.

Al made it to the end of the downstairs hall but then was stopped by a hand on his arm. It was Karen.

"Hey, buddy, where do you think you're going? Not so soon. It's hardly ten. You aren't getting out of here until you dance with me. I haven't felt a pair of arms like yours around me in, well, let's say a lot of years."

"I was just going to get some air, cool off a bit," he said, and looked away because of the lie.

"You can't fool me." She took his big hand and pressed it between hers. "You're running away from us and I don't blame you at all. The best thing about a party is the next day, when you know it's over and you can remember a few laughs anyway." She smiled and a wave of warmth washed over him so that he felt suddenly that he might kiss her, and looked dumbly at her, at her thin neck, her penciled eyebrows, her lined cheeks. Why, she's old, he thought and, amazed at himself, he put one arm around her shoulder and squeezed until she gasped and said, "Go along then!" and he rushed out into the snow.

The cold hit him like water. But instead of clearing his mind, it deepened his sense of being someone else tonight, someone other than Al Shafto, mechanic and bachelor bush rancher. The front walk was frothy and snow was still falling although, oddly, he could see stars. Stars and snow. It was like those strange days in spring when rain falls through bright sunlight so each drop shines. He had planned to stay at the Charlie Creek bunkhouse tonight but guessed he'd just go back to Bubbles, it was so early and the snow wasn't deep. He'd get there well before dawn. Breathing gratefully, his head light, he turned and saw a shadow cross the curtain upstairs at Bill and Marlene's.

It was Marlene, he knew this, even though the shadow was already gone. She, too, had sneaked away early. He took a step toward the house. Was she still wearing the blue dress? He had been jealous of Lanny's hand on her waist, Lanny who had more girls than he knew what to do with down at Fort St. John.

He was at Marlene's door. He opened the door, closed it behind him, and stood silent in the entry hall.

"Bill?"

Al didn't answer.

"Bill, is that you?"

He heard light footsteps overhead and something tripped inside him, fell in dizziness, made his heart thunder. Marlene was at the top of the stairs in a white bathrobe. She came down, stepping quickly in feet that were bare inside those see-through stockings that women wear. Walking straight to him, she slipped her arms around his middle and leaned her forehead against his chest. Al closed his arms and pressed to him the soft body, the white robe, the blonde hair that smelled of flowers.

When Bill came home, the last, with Skip, to leave the party, he found them asleep on his bed, Marlene curled in her slip with her head on Al's chest, Al on his back, fully dressed except for his boots. Bill had fallen down between the two houses. Unable to find the sidewalk under the new snow, he crawled to his porch on numb hands and came inside without brushing off. Gripping the newel post he hauled himself upright and stamped upstairs in his boots.

He stood in the bedroom doorway, hands red, snow melting down his neck, and gaped at his bed, his own bed with his own wife lying there practically naked beside the big bush ape.

Al's eyes opened and for a long moment he returned Bill's look with no particular expression. Then he lifted Marlene's head from his chest, swung his feet to the floor, and stood tall as a moose beside the bed. Bill moved aside and Al walked out of the room, down the stairs, and out into the night. He stepped from the small roofed porch into the snow, took two strides, and stopped, startled into sharp awareness by the strange sensation in his feet. He was walking in snow in nothing but socks. Soft and silent like cat's paws padding over carpet. Maybe he'd roll in the snow the way he'd done as a kid, his gray wool sweater and cut-down wool pants coming up fluffy as a lamb.

145

Sudden iciness in one heel made him stop. That hole in his sock. Damn. He sprang lightly back to the porch, eased open the door, and reached inside for his boots.

They were not in the entry hall. The wood floor was bare except for a mat, a pair of child's slippers, and two puddles forming around clumps of snow he knew without thinking had come in with Bill. It was hard to believe. After a lifetime of leaving his footwear at the door, he must have walked upstairs and down the hall, crossing Marlene's glassy floors with his dirty boots on. He would have to retrieve them—a sound made him go very still, listening. It came again, a low cry.

He leaped for the stairs and was up them in three bounds. He strode through the open door and across to the bed where Bill was slamming his fist down on Marlene's hands as they covered her face. Seizing Bill by the shoulders, Al dragged him from the bed and flung his blunt body across the room.

Bill smashed into a dresser, shattering the mirror on stop. He staggered, shook himself, and charged Al with his head down. Al's fist came up, catching him in the face and flinging him back so hard he landed in a wooden rocking chair and flipped it over backward. For a moment he lay stunned, but then crawled free and got to his feet. Swaying, one hand pressed to his bleeding nose, he turned to Marlene.

Marlene had not moved, Silent, her face also bleeding, she simply looked at her husband.

Seeing the blood on Marlene's hair, Al started for Bill again but stopped after two steps. He couldn't hit him when he was just standing there holding his face and rocking on his feet.

"How bad hurt are you?" he said to Marlene.

"It's just a cut," she said through her fingers. "You better go."

By the next evening, the episode had been hashed over in every house and trailer at Charlie Creek Station. Bill was in bed with a swollen nose and a painful back, and Marlene tended to Sammy and Danny with a puffy eye and a bandage on her left cheek. No one went out of the Kerly house and no one went in except for Karen, who had a whispered talk with Marlene in the entry hall around noon.

Al Shafto had gone back to Bubbles without talking to a soul, to finish his ten-day shift.

Bill stayed home for a week, but on the Monday after Christmas, Skip Pool stopped in front of the Kerly house the way he had just about every workday morning for the past eight years, lit a smoke, and waited. After a bit Bill came out, stooping a little as though carrying a weight, his earmuffs pulled low, his eye ringed with purple.

"Hey, Bill, good to see you." Skip did not smile. "You sure you're up to workin'?"

Bill grunted. For the length of the sidewalk, past the other four houses, they walked in silence. Karen waved from her front window. Skip waved back with a grin but Bill walked with his face straight ahead.

"That sonofabitch," he said as they turned up the short road to the pumping station. "Next time I lay eyes on that bastard—Jesus!" It was only a two-minute walk up the frozen road but in that two minutes, Bill told Skip in detail just what he was going to do to Shafto if he caught him showing his chicken-shit face around Charlie Creek any time soon. There wouldn't be enough of him left for his own mother to know him. The sonofabitching coward had caught him half asleep and drunk besides, but it would be different face to face and sober as witches, by Christ.

It was well below zero. Bill's breath shot out in a pulsing white stream as he talked and he flung his right arm about so wildly that Skip moved aside to keep from being hit. Bill held his left arm stiff, but by the time they reached the station he no longer stooped. He was a new man.

Skip and Bill entered the coffee room side-by-side through the double doors, and there was Al Shafto sitting against the wall, his big hands wrapped like a bun around a mug. Skip stepped quickly out of the way, but Bill merely nodded and said, "Hi, Al." And then, for the first time in eight years, he walked right on through to the engine room without stopping for coffee.

By eleven, Shafto had gone and Bill was back to warming the bench, but he didn't have much to say. He went home for lunch, as usual, but when he shouted for Marlene she came only as far as the bottom of the stairs, paintbrush in hand.

"I'm painting, Bill," she said, looking up through her good eye. She returned to the studio.

Bill Kerly stood for almost a minute watching the empty stairs, then he went to the kitchen to plug in the kettle for his tea.

Three Points of Contact

There's nothing like lying flat on the ground, heels planted, shoulders fixed, the flat weight of you steady against the globe. You feel earth along your spine. You sight up the trunk of a soaring Douglas fir tree at the sky. You feel calm and in place, and it strikes you that the moldering bodies buried all through this grove don't have it so bad.

To Tim's right lies Niklas Borloff, 1832-1906. To his left lies Maria Stanish Borloff, 1838-1905. He has already photographed the two headstones, not because they are handsome or picturesque—they're not—but because of the dates. The Borloffs died a year apart. Tim likes this and doesn't see it often in the older cemeteries. Too often the women go early, snatched away in childbirth, but Maria Stanish lived a full 67 years and Niklas, bereft, followed a year later.

Tim feels the sweetness of these proximal deaths. If he died first, would Lindsey pine for him, and fade away until she found a place by his side? No. He rolls his head on the grass, negative. She would stick around for the girls. He's sure of this, and smiles. If you have to play second fiddle in your wife's affections, it may as well be to your own spawn.

But it would be different if Lindsey were to die first. He would follow her to the grave like a kitten following the cream. The two of them would lie like this forever, side-by-side into eternity, trees shooting straight up from their bones.

What would Lindsey say if he were to propose buying two funeral plots here?

If that's what you want, but wouldn't it be better to wait until the girls are through college?

He would praise the location to her, talk it up like a new house. *It's an intimate little place, a long way out from town, musical breezes blowing, a privileged spot to lie down forever.*

Walking about with his camera earlier, pulling away chunks of moss to read inscriptions and then carefully patching the moss back into place after the photo was done, he had played a game he often played in cemeteries. He had pretended that his mother was buried here. His mother was buried by the sundial on the far side of the graveyard where it dropped away to the valley, and when he arrived at that spot he would kneel by her side and remember when they'd camped in the summer and she'd cooked biscuits in a Dutch oven.

He didn't remember the Dutch oven but he had seen pictures. He didn't remember much about his childhood in general, and least of all about the later years, after she started drinking. The obvious explanation was that he had blotted the memories out in self-protection, but what about the happy early years, why could he not remember those?

His sister Elaine, four years older, could talk on and on about childhood adventures, while he had only the faintest glimmerings of what might be memories but also might simply be triggered by the pictures his father had taken and put into albums back when people made albums. The pictures had stuck in his mind rather than the real thing.

Was this what drove him to photograph his own Molly and Mira compulsively? Along with everything else that moved him, including graveyards?

He wants to remember more. He wants to remember his mother,

not as she was in the final, furious years but as she was when she played with them on the beach, and did cookouts, and read *Treasure Island* and then made elaborate treasure hunts—or so Elaine said.

Lying among the graves it seems to him that if only he had a place to go to feel close to his mother he could get the memories back. He raises himself onto one elbow and gazes down into the grass, the ground, the lodging place. Does it really matter where he goes to remember? He shouldn't need a grave to help him remember. In all his years of photographing cemeteries, how many people had he encountered sitting next to the graves of their loved ones, remembering?

Not one. Not a single one.

But to have his father on one side and his mother on the other, and to lie like this on the ground between them, remembering. . . The fantasy makes him feel greedy. God has nothing to do with it. Faith and spirit have nothing to do with it. It would be good in itself, and he thinks with envy of the Borloff children, if they exist somewhere, and hopes that they come here sometimes and aren't indifferent to their good luck.

Where can he go to try to reclaim the closeness to his mother that he must have felt once, that Elaine insisted he had felt, that he craved to feel again, even in memoriam. Where was she? Why had they all been so helpless when she died? All of them, doing nothing, not talking about it, acting as though it hadn't happened or as though she had done something wicked and unforgivable to them all for dying at 49.

His father had taken care of the ashes, had put them in the river, he said. His mother had been set adrift on a current that ran to the sea.

Tim sits up, rubbing his elbow and squinting in the light. Molly has appeared from behind a blackened stone angel leading Mira by the hand, the two of them in dresses, barefoot among the headstones.

"Will you die?" Mira asks Molly.

"Yes," says Molly.

"Will I die?"

"Yes."

"Will Mommy die?"

"Yes."

"Will Daddy die?"

"Yes."

"Will Auntie Elaine die?"

"Yes."

"We'll all die." Mira, it appears, is pleased by the tidiness of it.

"But we won't go to heaven," says Molly.

"Where will we go?"

"To be dead," Molly replies, as calm as day.

Tim opens his arms and gathers them to him, smelling grass in their hair. "Your grandmother would have loved you very much," he says.

"Grandma's not in a grave," says Molly.

"No, she's not in a grave," Tim says, surprised. Has he really talked about this to his young daughters?

"We don't want a grave, do we Mira?" Molly says.

Mira shakes her head.

"You could go anywhere when you're dead," says Molly. "We're going in a treehouse."

"Is Grandma in a treehouse?" Mira looks up into the tall Douglas fir.

Tim smiles and is ready to answer, but no words form. He has no response to this question. He, too, looks up the soaring trunk. The tree has grown out in the open, without crowding, and its multitudinous branches start low. He could easily climb it. He could climb it like stairs. . . And there she is, suddenly, his mother just above him in a tree and saying mildly, *Remember to keep three points of contact whenever you climb anything. If a branch breaks you'll still be fine.* It

154

is not a memory created by a picture, it's a real memory. He wants to laugh but holds back, caught by two serious gazes fixed on him, waiting.

"Is she?" Mira says again.

"Yes, yes, very likely so. Grandma's up a tree," he says. "She liked trees a lot. We could get pretty far up this one, I think. Let's try it, okay? You're big enough to reach. Just remember to keep three points of contact at all times. Then you'll be fine no matter what happens."

Tim leads the way, showing them which branches to step on, where to take hold with their right hands, their left hands.

"It's sticky," Mira says when she's about six feet up.

"That's because of pitch." Molly sits on a thick branch just above her sister's head and swings one bare foot.

"You don't have any contact on that foot," Mira says. "Daddy! Molly doesn't have any contact on her foot."

Tim is well above them now and doesn't want to stop. He looks up at the dark network of branches against the sky, and then down on their shaggy heads. Molly is not only swinging her foot but has let go with one hand to do something with a twig.

"Molly, what are you doing? Why aren't you holding on?"

"It's pitch," she says, not looking up. "It's like honey. Can I eat it?"

"No," he says. "You should hold on with both hands."

"I'm sitting down," she says, continuing to probe with the twig. "A bug's stuck in it. I'm getting him out."

"Stop that and hold on," he says. "Now."

As always happens with children there is no warning. Molly does not even cry out. One moment she is sitting in the tree, the next she's on the ground. It's Mira who screams.

Tim drops through the tree without any sense of climbing, moving too fast to think about feet and hands and proper holds. He drops to the ground, landing soft on the fir needle duff, and folds onto his knees with no break in movement. Molly lies curled on her left side, her dress twisted, her hair over her face. He lifts the hair with a shaking hand.

His oldest daughter's eyes are fully open and staring. They blink. "Molly?"

"I can't breathe."

Of course she's breathing or she wouldn't be able to speak, but he says, "Don't try to talk. Your breath will come back."

Where does it hurt? Why didn't you hold on? Why didn't you keep three points of contact? I thought you were reliable. . . He doesn't say anything more for the moment. He stands up and lifts Mira down, and together they sit under the tree watching and waiting for Molly to tell them all about it. How old was he when he climbed the tree with his mother? Six? Seven? Did he always keep three points of contact, then and forever after in all the trees he'd climbed in his life? No, of course not. He'd never fallen but that was just luck. *We do our best. You did your best, Mom. I do my best for my daughters, your granddaughters.*

After a bit Molly sits up and looks around as though to see who else might have observed the fall, but only the gravestones stand scattered about on lumpy grass. "I didn't cry," she says, and hitches sideways to get into her father's lap.

"It's okay to cry," he says, and hears the words as an echo. *It's okay to cry, sweetie, truly it's okay to cry.* He doesn't see her this time but he knows now who's speaking in his mind and he nods, then shakes his head. "But it's good not to, if you can help it. You know what they've discovered? It turns out you feel better if you smile."

"I fell out of the tree," she says as though to remind him.

"Yes, yes, of course. I didn't mean you should smile now. But maybe crying actually makes us feel worse, like not smiling."

"Did you get the bug?" says Mira.

"What?" Molly sits up in her father's lap to look at her sister.

"Did you get the bug?"

"The bug in the pitch," Tim says, and urges the girls to their feet.

Molly brushes off her dress and takes her father's hand. "If I got killed falling down I could be buried here."

"We don't want to be buried," says Mira.

"If I could have an angel it would be okay."

They set off across the cemetery. Tim stoops to pick up his camera bag, not letting go of Molly's hand. The girls had been in at least forty cemeteries in their short lives, had played on many a grave and been photographed on many a sarcophagus. It was enough—too much, no doubt—and it was time to move on.

"Remember, three points of contact at all times," he says, and Mira instantly bends at the waist to walk on one hand and two legs.

"You can't fall off the ground," Molly says, musing as though there might be some question about this.

"Nope," says her father. "You won't fall off the ground. That is one thing in life that you can be pretty darned sure about."

The Red Birdfeeder

The day before she was to begin her trip around the world, Melba Siebert sat at the kitchen table watching a scrub jay bully finches at the feeder, and it came to her with the nerveless clarity of revelation that Leland was right. She was doing a mad thing. She was, by her own will and wish, leaving this safe house on the hill. And it could happen that she would never return, not by her own decision, but through circumstances she could not even imagine as she sat looking beyond the feeder into oaks whose leaves she had watched bud, swell, and fall for 43 years. Once the tie was snapped, as it would have to be when she walked away from her door, everything would be out of her hands. She would have no control over anything, not even coffee. Her day was defined by coffee, coffee on the deck at daylight, coffee with toast, coffee to launch her out the door for her walk, coffee to mark that she was home again. Would they serve coffee or tea on the boat? Could she get coffee between meals? Would there be fresh milk? Would she be utterly at the mercy of ship routine? Had it been a mistake to insist on a freighter?

"You can't go, Mother." For the first time in years Leland had been impatient with her, almost angry. "It's not right, not on a freighter. Not at your age. That's a young person's lark." He would buy her a ticket on a liner, a luxury cruise with gourmet meals, entertainment, shops. "You'd love it, don't say you wouldn't."

"And you'd be off the hook for a Christmas present."

"Were you as stubborn with Dad as you are with James and me?"

"Cruises are for old people."

She did not want luxury. She did not want gourmet food. She had no use for shops, being more inclined to get rid of things than to acquire them since Dale died. And if it was popular entertainment she wanted, she would do better to stay at home with TV.

What else was she to do? She was too old for the Peace Corps, at least in spirit. She had volunteered enough at the library. The senior center offended her with its holiday parties and bingo nights, as though they were children. She had gone to the journal writing class a few times but the fellow students depressed her. The four old ladies— widows all—were sure they had led extraordinary lives that wanted only the proper telling. None had done a thing out of the ordinary that Melba could see.

No, a freighter was the thing. A working boat with room for just 12 passengers to travel simply, unburdened by organized fun but forced, at least, to converse because there would be too few to allow hiding. It was for only five weeks. Five weeks.

It was a long time.

It had to be done.

"I need something pushing me," she had insisted into the long-distance line, trying to make her boys understand. "There's nothing pushing me. I've stopped. I need a different world."

On the boat there would be routine. A time to get up, a time to eat, a time to talk and listen, a time to nap, a time to stand at the rail and watch the sky. And sneaking into this routine like a stray cat with wild eyes would come that unexpected something, that sudden opening of heart that makes you wonder that life ever could have seemed empty or fruitless or burdensome.

"I crave a change," she told James when he called on her birthday.

"You know I never liked repetition, and now my days are like white hankies folded up in a drawer, each one the same, each one spotless. I want some spots back in my life before it's too late."

"Spots? You would put it like that. But you aren't young anymore. You don't even know if there's a doctor on board."

A doctor! When she had truly needed a doctor on board was long ago, when James and Leland were in school and bringing home every bug that hit town. If she'd had doubts about this trip, they were settled now. To her boys she had become an old woman. But she was not frail. She had not had a cold or sore throat in years. No arthritis. No varicose veins. No osteoporosis. No obvious senility. Just boredom.

Boredom. Worse by far than senility!

Yes, she was bored. Here, in the same house where—once upon a time—every hour in the day had been a contest, a performance, a triumph over chaos, there was nothing to do now that couldn't wait a day, a week, forever.

Except for feeding the birds.

"What's all the ruckus about?" she said aloud. The jay, having vanquished the finches, now stared hard at her through the window from its perch on the deck railing. "Maybe I am getting senile."

She stood, opened the sliding door, and stepped out into air sharp with the tang of wet oak. Crossing the deck, she unhooked the birdfeeder, tipped it over the railing, and watched papery seed scraps drift down onto dark leaves speckled already with yesterday's seed bits, and those from the day before and the day before. Tomorrow she would be gone and Jeanie would take over this ritual. Jeanie would stump along the gravel path between their two houses, her legs thick as pilings. Breathing hard, clutching the wood railing, she would haul herself up the steps to the deck. Alone at last at Dale's house, she would pause to savor the moment before taking down the feeder.

Jeanie would handle the feeder with her fat hands. The feeder that Dale had made.

He had made it for Melba's birthday, a fanciful feeder shaped like a pagoda but painted bright red and green like a Scandinavian toy. Now it was richly mottled like old barn siding, the wood gray-brown and flecked with lichens. Dale, alive, would sand and paint it but Melba preferred it like this, earthy as a crusted stone. Nothing of her own choosing had ever been glossy, although she had been happy with the feeder, had not objected to the paint. Presents are always a little off, a little skewed from what one would choose, and this is part of the surprise and fun of it—although Jeanie, naturally, had made a big appreciative fuss, had said it was darling and touched it with a fingernail as red as the paint.

Red is sexy.

Dale had not cared much for sex. He told her so before they married and she said, "Fine, I don't care much about it myself."

It was work they both loved, and how they had worked in the early years! Dale at the university and in his wood shop downstairs, Melba with the boys, the house, and the feature writing job at the *News-Herald* when it came. Such energy they had then, such long and busy days followed by exhausted sleep. . . And then suddenly one night Dale had wanted her, really wanted her. Instead of reading, he lay naked on the bed watching her, and put his arms around her while she was undressing. After the first surprise, Melba had been pleased though not fooled. He was fending off middle age. Male menopause was scaring him into lust. Still, how pleasant it was to be wanted, and what a revelation to discover that she cared. It was almost embarrassing—talk about late bloomers.

Such a joke. Ignorance is bliss.

Melba looked through oak branches at the yellow corner of Jeanie's house and was surprised to feel something like a laugh wanting to surface. How long had it taken her to see the truth? Not long, and for this she was glad. Ignorance is not really bliss.

Dale and Melba had been the first couple to build on the hilltop.

They designed the house, milled their own paneling from native chinquapin, and then lived for years in pleasant seclusion among the old oaks until Skip and Jeanie bought the other lot. They bought the land in April and by August the contractors had finished and gone. Melba, trying to make the best of it, had invited the new neighbors for spaghetti. Had it started then, that first night, so very soon? Yes. Melba nodded. She believed it had, even though she had not consciously noted it and Dale had been rigidly proper in not looking at Jeanie's sleek legs—Melba had certainly looked! Dale had directed his talk to Skip despite the lack of sympathy between the men, Skip, a realtor, having zero interest in forest research except, maybe, to the extent that it might lead to cheaper lumber for houses. But Melba had soon felt the attraction in the same way she had always felt such dangerous links among their friends. The lines of desire were plain to her, plainer than her own feelings, even though she could not understand how Dale could fall for such a foolish woman, a woman who answered thank you letters because she had nothing better to do.

For a while, dismayed, Melba had avoided her neighbors. But something inside her refused to keep up the game. A marriage tie is such an accident, a small click in the universe when two people come together at a certain moment in their lives and become stuck, bonded like atoms even though they might be as different as sodium and chloride. And she had discovered a need in herself that, newly awakened, would not go away. She wanted Dale's desire, even if it really was meant for someone else.

She invited Skip and Jeanie to dinner parties and seated Jeanie next to Dale. She arranged picnics and watched Dale try not to watch Jeanie in her turquoise swimsuit. She gave barbecues and assigned Dale and Jeanie to mind the grill while she heated garlic bread and made drinks in the kitchen. And after they waved their neighbors home from the dark porch, her pleasure was complex when Dale reached for her right there in the night as though they were 17.

Skip and Dale were both long gone, leaving the hilltop to the two women. What if Melba and Skip had died first and left Dale and Jeanie alone on the hill? Would it have mattered to Dale that Jeanie was now fat and limped?

Melba smacked the bottom of the feeder, shook it, carried it to the laundry room, filled it with seeds, returned it to the hanger.

Yesterday, standing with one hand on the mailbox, her thick body slightly bent as it always was now, Jeanie had been amazed. "You're not packed yet? I was packed two weeks before our cruise. But you've always been so cool-minded."

Cool-minded? Was she cool-minded? What is a cool mind?

But she would pack now. It was time.

Entering the living room from the hall, Melba reached to snap on a light but stopped, her hand poised near the switch. Let it stay dark. It had always been dim in this room. The wood paneling soaked up what light got through the oaks and the Douglas firs that cast shade even in winter. In here, you wouldn't know it was spring. They had never spent much time in this room except when company came. They had done no living in the living room. Melba lived in the kitchen, the laundry room, the garden, her tiny study. Dale, when he was home, was in his wood shop. The boys were outdoors or in the big room downstairs where they could do anything except start fires.

Melba sat on the couch. She sat still and nothing moved. The room was dead. There was not a sound, not even ticking. After Dale died—absurdly young, not even gray—she had removed the clocks, the ticking clocks, the chiming clocks, the musical clocks. He had made them all, sanding the wood to satin, always making them as presents but never, in the end, giving a single one away. This had been left for her to do and hadn't James been shocked. "Mother, you can't—" how they loved that word! "—you can't get rid of Dad's clocks. It's like he never existed."

A clock is not a man. Books are not a man. A man is a certain crunch of gravel on a dark driveway. A man is the smell of shirts in the laundry.

She listened. A distant siren wailed. Noon already. By noon she had always had life ordered, Dale and the boys off to work and school, clothes washing, chicken thawing, blouse ironed, calls made, and she would be free to set off driving in search of feature story ideas. She hadn't been a real reporter. She never cared about news. There is nothing new. She wanted people stories, human stories, the stories that never change, the man who lived alone back in the hills with his seeing-eye pig, the woman in labor on the roof of the barn where she had escaped with her family when the Long Tom River flooded. What tireless drive she'd had then, what humor—Melba stood abruptly, walked to the front door, put her hand on the knob, paused. It was too early for mail. And there would be no letter. No one wrote letters now. James had sent his weekly email note two days early because of her trip and Leland never wrote, he phoned, whatever he had to say needing to be blurted at once just as it always had, no time to wait even for her to finish in the bathroom but pounding on the door and shouting.

The front porch was empty apart from a cedar planter. In a different spring it would hold marigolds. She had put out no bedding plants this year. They would need water, and she was tired of marigolds. Tired of petunias, tired of impatiens, tired of nicotiana, all of them spindly and unhappy under the oaks. She wanted big, luscious hibiscus blooms and bougainvillea dripping from white stucco archways. The ship would be white-hot as they crossed the southern oceans and when it docked, smells of peppery cooking and warm stone would drift over the deck.

Had she swept the porch that morning? There was not a leaf on it. She wasn't sure, she didn't think she had swept it, but it was amazingly—terribly—clean, the green-tinted concrete as simple as something new with not one trace left of the pounding tennis shoes, the skates, the spilled jack-o-lantern wax, the chalk from Leland's fling at sidewalk art. All cleared away without a hint of that life left behind.

Melba put a steadying hand on the door molding. She needed to eat. There was time. She could pack later. The limousine would pick her up at eight, a decent hour, and for five weeks she would think of nothing but what passed before her eyes as the ship steamed across endless seas. She wouldn't write, she knew she wouldn't. The writing was a pretext. I need fresh material, she had told the boys. I've written everything that ever happened to me—absurd.

Absurd! Melba slammed the wide front door and then stood in the hall frozen among echoes.

Dale had always been first up in the morning, the door slamming behind him being her signal to reach for her robe even though she was usually awake long before he went. She lay awake half the night, her body tight with thoughts and emotions she could not control in that passive posture. She hated the night, hated lying stiff and anxious with the world shut down around her, unable to secure all the rope ends that flapped in her mind. James had not been doing his eye exercises, Leland's breathing was bad again from the allergies, his bedroom air cleaner needed a new filter, the battery in the boys' smoke alarm was old, she had forgotten to pick up the tickets to the play—all so trivial but it added up to failure despite the furious energy that drove her through the days. There was something missing in her. She was not a proper woman, she could not keep it all smooth and cozy. The family rampart stood on hollow ground.

And yet, once the door slammed behind Dale, she would leap out of bed before his car started, full of the relief that only action brings. Move, move, move, there is nothing like getting it done to quell the night dragons.

"So absurd," she said. "I thought I wanted peace."

She had fought for order and balance. In the mornings, in her robe, she had gone from room to room turning off the stark overhead lights that Dale clicked on as he passed through and then did not notice again. She closed the door to the downstairs to keep out drafts, closed the hall door so the cat—which always sneaked past Dale, who claimed never to see her—wouldn't wake the boys, gathered the day's newspaper pages from the back of the toilet, the hall table, and the kitchen counter into one stack, turned off the kitchen radio and turned on the kitchen lamp, cleared Dale's plate and cup away, screwed the lid on the jam, poured out the half pot of burned coffee and put on fresh, and opened the blind so she could see the dawn.

"Sometimes I think you'd like to wipe out all traces of me," Dale had said once, chuckling. "I'm just another messy kid in your life."

A table with a bouquet, afternoon wind heard through a window, sun blinking behind black oak limbs, the unified chorus of crickets, words rising in her like the purest air. This had been Melba's dream. It had not been a dream with room for more than one.

You have the most powerful double life line I've ever seen, the palmist told her long before she met Dale. *You lead an intense inner life that is separate from your outer life but you must have both to be happy*. A powerful double life? What nonsense. She had far more than that, a hundred lives, a hundred uncertainties, a hundred questions about how to be. Who could possibly have only two selves? An imbecile.

How many selves had lived inside Dale?

"You don't love Dad, do you?" Leland had looked at her with wounded adolescent eyes.

"Love your father?" They did not often use the word love in this family. Children say I hate you and in the next breath I love you, but no adult can honestly use such terms. Melba had not said I love you even when she married Dale. She never said I love you to her boys, although as she watched them sleep her heart choked her with its fullness and she would have died for them gladly.

"I don't know exactly what love is," she had said to Leland, knowing it wouldn't do. "But I think we have a good marriage, don't you?"

"You're being evasive. You don't want to admit it but I can see it. You never kiss him."

"Kissing is private for our generation."

"I don't mean just kissing. I mean all that goes along with it. Affection. You never hug him or anything and you don't like it when he talks when you're reading. Your feet wiggle."

"Does he hug me?"

Leland had looked around, confused, and Melba had seen him thinking that he had blundered, that he should have considered that hugs and kisses go two ways.

"I used up all my hugs and kisses on you when you were little," she had teased, but he wouldn't laugh.

"I don't think you love him. I think you should love him."

"Do you think he loves me?"

"Sure he does. You're his wife."

She was his wife. He was her husband. For 31 years they had performed in concert, a domestic vaudeville team. But had she loved him? How could she love him when, watching and listening to the figure that was called Dale, she must wonder how many layers were hidden from her like so much of her was hidden from him, the shifting internal sands so often obscuring even her own view of herself. He could not know her. How could she pretend to know him?

Melba could not imagine anyone loving except blindly, as a child loves. How easy it had been to love her babies! But year after year, the layers sealed those babies deeper inside until they had become as unknowable as actors or foreigners. "Don't you feel you hardly know Jamie in that mustache?" Jeanie had asked her when James came back from his second year at medical school. "I haven't known him since he was four," Melba had replied, and Jeanie laughed at her joke.

Oh, the boys loved her, of course they did. They were attentive, James wrote, Leland called, they gave a lot of thought to presents. When she died they would suffer and their feelings for a few days would be terribly real. But Leland didn't even remember Bombs Away. She had played the game with him for hours every day before he was old enough for school, her town of blocks on one side of the rug, his on the other, taking turns with their improvised catapults, firing, making great booming noises with each shot whether it hit or not.

"I didn't know any other mother who worked," James had said a while ago. "It's funny I didn't notice it then but I suppose you were ahead of your time. They all work now."

"But I didn't work when you were little," she had protested. "And never full time."

Dale was in full career swing then, but she was always home when her boys got home, always driving to lessons and making pancakes or French toast—no damned cornflakes!—but in what had seemed like no time at all she had found herself wandering a silent house, watering plants, washing dish towels that weren't dirty, starting dinner too early because her boys needed nothing from her but the evening meal. They'll need money for college, she had decided when both were in high school, and increased her hours at the *News-Herald*, writing up to five features a week instead of three. When she had apologized, explaining the need for extra money, Leland had said only, "Does that mean the car won't be here in the afternoons?"

There was no food in the refrigerator. She had not shopped for five days, not wanting to have to deal with leftover lettuce or eggs. She could not throw food out even now and there was no point in passing anything along to Jeanie. She ate from cans and boxes, never real food, even when Skip was alive.

Melba would eat from the freezer, clear that mess out a bit. She looked into the small cave of ice and saw jammed into one piece juices, peas, bones waiting to be soup, a granite chicken. She took out the only loose package, a Danish of unknown age, not a good one by the look of it but a cheapie from the bakery at Fairway. It must have been left from the last journal writing meeting, which she had offered to hold here as a sort of apology for quitting. They all said she had such promise. And she was so productive. Standing by the refrigerator with the cold pastry in hand, Melba looked at her typewriter on the kitchen table and, surprised, saw that it was swamped by papers that covered the table except for the little bay where she ate meals. How had this come to be? How could she have strayed so far from the days when she needed order so desperately she wouldn't waste time pestering the boys—and Dale—to pick up after themselves but did it for them, stuffing books, balls, socks, and papers alike into baskets she had placed in every room for just this purpose.

The baskets were gone now but, inexplicably, so was her need for order. The table that had been a prime neatness battleground was now mounded with bills, ad circulars, catalogs, books, drawings by Leland's kids. . . She dropped the Danish onto a plate, shoved it into the microwave, and filled the kettle.

Tearing the sticky roll into fragments, Melba watched the sky beyond the oak limbs change from blue to bright gray. The clouds thickened and darkened. Her coffee was cold. She heated it for thirty seconds and carried it to the bedroom to drink while she packed.

A single suitcase, her typewriter, Dale's old briefcase for the manuscript she wouldn't work on. This was all she would allow herself. There had to be a laundry on board. Two cotton slacks, one skirt, four blouses, shorts, sweater, windbreakers, stockings and socks, shampoo. Melba packed fast, pulling clothes from drawers and closet with no thought. She had decided weeks ago to travel as she had during college when she cycled around Europe before it became a youth cliché, when it was still considered not quite seemly for a girl to be on her own. Slim, square-faced, rarely cold, she had needed very little to get by, had taken pride in being handsome because of the blood in her cheeks rather than the cut of her blouse or hair, which was short and straight.

"You're so liberated," Jeanie had said more than once. "I never went anywhere until I got married."

Liberated!

Melba sat down on the hard twin bed. Liberated? She had been a terrible prude. Watching old men feed pigeons at Trafalgar Square, she had felt a presence behind her and turned to find a gaunt young man in a kilt. His nose and chin were keels, his cheeks red like a five-year-old's, his blue eyes obsessive but bright with fun. They had talked of pigeons, of music, of cycling, of Scotland where he would return when he finished school, and all the while she had wanted to giggle at the sight of his startling, naked male knees. They had ordered tea nearby and at twilight as he saw her onto the bus back to her hostel, he had asked for her London address and suggested a picnic, his low voice rumbly and shy. Her hand on the humming metal of the door, she had flushed hot. But I don't know you. We were not properly introduced, one does not take up seriously with strange men in parks, even in London.

Absurd girl!

What if she had gone for the picnic?

The thought, a heavy weight, pushed her back until she lay on the hard bed and closed her eyes, her thin arms bare on the cotton bedspread, her body inconsequential. Leland and Jamie might be half someone else. She could not imagine it.

She had returned to London years later with Dale, after the boys finished school. Trafalgar Square had been salted with trash and pigeon droppings and the young men were all in black. Where was her Scot today? A bent old man wearing thermals under his kilt. Dead under the ground of a raw moor. But she could not see him bent or wrinkled. She could only see him looking down at her with flaming cheeks. How many of her layers would he have seen through with that straight blue gaze? And the others over the years, the brief touches, the conversations, the eyes that were so instantly familiar they might have been her own except that they watched her from a man's face. In a different time and life, what might any one of these have become to her? We marry and in an instant we shut a hundred gates to who knows what gardens. And yet, would she not choose Dale a second time?

Melba slept and hours later woke, shivering, on top of the covers, her breathing tight in the solid dark that had somehow filled the world. Leland Jamie Dale! She nearly cried aloud—but remembered they were gone and nothing remained but this, herself on a bed in a dark and silent room. There is nothing undone, nothing to do. I am supposed to sleep now.

But she did not sleep. Ten minutes, twenty minutes, half an hour.

She got up, put on her robe, walked out to the dark deck, took down the feeder and pressed it to her chest. It was the last thing Dale had made on this earth, a birdfeeder for her birthday, the feeder she had filled every day for years without number. They had married, they had made a life, they had loved, loved so many things.

In the morning she would write a note to Jeanie saying never mind. The birds can make do for five weeks.

Smiling tenderly, cradling the feeder, Melba Siebert went back into the house to finish packing for her trip around the world.

Birthday Moon

Eric's rejection of his fourteenth birthday dinner could have ruined Friday evening for the Arden family, but his mother remembered just in time that it was, after all, Eric's birthday and not the family's.

"Fine. Go to the game," she said. "We'll do it tomorrow."

So they waited a day to prepare the meal that Eric had requested: shrimp Louie, garlic bread, and chocolate cream pie. Vera said it was a lot of candles for one pie but she let Callie, eight, sink them nearly to the wicks in whipped cream. The candles burned well enough anyway, and Eric blew them out with a show of heroic effort.

"Whew, that was tough," he said, and wiped his brow to keep Callie laughing.

His father had chopped the vegetables for the Louie and made the garlic butter but even so he volunteered to wash the dishes for his birthday boy, whose turn it would have been in the normal KP rotation. He dried the plates, his coffee cup on the windowsill, while Eric sprawled on his back on the living room rug. Through two walls, Paul could feel his son trying to reason out how long he had to remain downstairs to keep from hurting everyone's feelings before escaping to his room to call the girl he'd talked to last night instead of watching the game.

I could let him off the hook with a word. . . Paul looked out the window and saw a half moon hanging clear-cut and golden in the late evening sky. There had been talk of Pictionary, ping pong, maybe a fire, but the rains were coming and such nights as this were numbered.

"There's a wonderful moon," he said, turning to his wife. "Let's go out to Barn Hill."

Vera stepped to his side, looked out, and nodded even as she said, "I don't think Callie's up to walking so soon after her cold."

"We don't have to walk. We could see the moon from the little meadow past the barn."

"I'm game if the kids want to." She headed into the living room and within seconds he heard his daughter's long-drawn-out cry.

"Noooooooooo."

And then Eric's voice. "I don't really feel like it. I'm too tired. Sorry if that makes you mad but I'd rather stay here."

"I'm not mad," said Vera.

"You are mad. I can tell."

"I'm not mad," Vera said again with perfect patience. "You don't have to go."

Paul crossed the small dining room to stand in the arched doorway the living room. "It's your birthday," he said. "We don't have to go. We'll stay here. How about some ping pong?"

"No, it's okay. You want to go. Mom wants to go. We'll go."

"I don't want to go." Callie ran from the room and halfway up the stairs before collapsing with her head on her crossed arms.

"She's just tired," said Vera. "She'll be fine."

Vera got warm clothes for Callie, rolled up a blanket, put on her jacket, zipped Callie's jacket, urged the cat out the back door. Paul, as usual, was ready first and stood outside the front door waiting to lock up.

"Where's Eric?" he said when his wife and daughter came out.

"He's not in the car?"

Returning to the living room, Paul found his son barefoot, in ripped shorts, deep in a fantasy novel, his long legs stretched between the couch and the hassock.

"We're leaving."

"I decided not to go." Eric did not look up from the book.

"Fine," Paul said and turned back toward the door. He knew this game too well to bite on the bait.

"Just kidding!" Eric bounced up off the couch, as Paul had known he would.

You never really know, though, he mused. *There could be a first time. There's sure to be a first time.*

Eric reached down beside the couch and retrieved his sweatshirt and a blanket. Cradling them, he followed his father out the door.

"No shoes?" said Paul.

"Oh, ha ha." Eric turned back to collect his sandals from the hall closet. The last time the Ardens went backpacking he had arrived at the trailhead with no shoes, having forgotten to put them into the car, he said, because they'd left too early to think.

Callie was already in the van sitting at the near end of the bench seat, blocking the door.

"Move over!" growled Eric.

"Don't touch me."

"Let me in then."

"Gently, gently," Vera said from the front seat. "Callie, move over."

"Can I use that blanket?" said Callie.

"No, I brought it."

"It's my blanket."

"No, it's not. Anyway, I only have shorts on so I need it."

"You could have worn long pants like the rest of us." Paul looked over his shoulder as he backed out of the driveway. "It shouldn't get too cold anyway."

Barn Hill Park, four miles west of town, was an oak-covered bump on the valley floor. The weathered old barn that belonged to the original farm overlooked the small gravel parking area. As the car turned in, Vera whispered sharply, "Deer!"

A doe stood in the headlights. She strolled away as they watched and sprang lightly over the fence that stood between the park and the neighboring farm field.

"If I ever drew a deer," Vera said, "I'd never think to draw it with such a small head."

"That's why they're so dumb," said Eric.

"The largest brain ever measured came from a person with Down syndrome," Paul said.

"What's that?" asked Callie.

"It means retarded but you aren't supposed to say that," said Eric. "There's nobody here."

Apart from their van the lot was empty, which was not surprising given the late hour, the October coolness, and the thin cloud that had now dulled the moon.

"Don't touch any bushes," Paul reminded them as they strung out single file on the path. "There's poison oak everywhere."

The path led past the barn and then split, one branch curving darkly off to the left to climb the hill, the other leading straight ahead to contour around the base of the hill through a meadow. Against the blue-black sky the gable of the barn was a night sail.

"Not many of these old barns left," said Paul, speaking low. "They're marvelous. Very, very—" he broke off, searching for the word.

"Devotional," said Vera.

"Yes, devotional. That's good." Paul nodded in the dark.

"I wish I could get closer to you." Callie shrank against Vera's leg as they passed the black door of the barn.

"You couldn't get any closer unless you got inside my skin." Vera placed a hand on her daughter's warm head.

Paul led the way along the lower trail. To see the moon they would have to leave the trail and cross the meadow toward the dark line of ash and willows that followed the creek. The crickets were active tonight with that extra intensity that comes late in the season, and as the Ardens walked the sound pulled back in a ring around them. They veered off the trail. The tarweed, bent underfoot, sent up a resin smell sharp enough to taste. The ground heaved with anthills, molehills, and gopher holes, but the unevenness was softened by tall grass that had been beaten down and matted by the first autumn rain.

It was dry now, and when Paul knelt to check with his hand, he found it warm and springy. "This is good," he said, and unrolled the blanket. Stretched out on his back he looked up at the stars but saw only the silhouettes of Vera and Callie.

"I want to wrap up in the blanket," Callie said, not quite whining.

"Is the ground wet?" asked Vera. "We should have brought more blankets."

"It's perfectly dry." Paul rolled off and waited on his knees while Vera stooped for the blanket, wrapped their daughter like a Tootsie roll, and helped her to lie down. Vera sat beside her for a moment and then she too stretched out flat, looking up. Paul rested on his back a few feet away and Eric settled himself up the slope about twenty feet from them.

"Why don't you come down with us?" Vera called softly.

"I like it here," he said. "You guys are too noisy."

"Hear the coyote?" Vera whispered to her daughter. "Or it might be a fox. Both can make a sort of barking sound like that."

"Do foxes hurt?"

"Hurt?"

"People."

"Heavens no. They're just little and shy, like a big cat."

They lay at the edge of the tilted meadow with the dark slope of

Barn Hill on one side and the line of wetland trees on the other. Cradling his head on his arms, Paul looked up at a thin wash of stars. He saw the flat-sided moon lodge in the branches of a tall tree on the hill so that the feathered arms seemed to expand and vibrate. Branches and crickets hummed together.

It is night, it is fall, and he is poised, ready for revelation, ready for that moment when he will forget his solid body that presses into the grass and, thoughtless, become pure meadow, sky, and stars. Crickets, black hill, moonlight. . . How he loves it. How refreshing it is. But it comes to him lying there under the sky that he is not going to be swept away by pure sensation even if he waits all night, no, not swept away as a poet must be or as he had been at twenty, so hungry then for deeps of every kind. *What have I lost? When did I lose it?*

Uncertain, wary of disappointment, he hears a new sound, small and regular and not far away. Snoring.

His daughter, rolled in the cotton blanket, is snoring against her mother's side. Vera is silent, motionless, a piece of the ground. Eric could be a stone. He himself hasn't moved in—he has no idea how long. The moon has slid far along the ridge from that tall tree, the crickets have done, the air is colder and carries a hint of wet from the creek.

We lie here on the ground, we four, and listen and dream and sleep. My children—even the boy at new, uneasy 14—know how to be still under the stars, how to stretch out on top of October grass and melt away.

It wouldn't do for a poet, no, probably not. But it's fine, just fine, and he nods drowsily at the cloud-dimmed October moon.

Wendy Madar is the co-author of the photography memoir *Through Another Lens: My Years with Edward Weston* (Farrar, Straus & Giroux, 1998) and, writing as Ashna Graves, the author of two mysteries, *Death Pans Out* (Poisoned Pen Press, 2007) and *No Angel* (Lychgate Press, 2012). She lives in Oregon.

www.ingramcontent.com/pod-product-compliance
Lightning Source LLC
Chambersburg PA
CBHW050731250626
47155CB00005B/1753